George Washington Kettoman

The Lady of Winderslee

George Washington Kettoman

The Lady of Winderslee

ISBN/EAN: 9783337054601

Printed in Europe, USA, Canada, Australia, Japan

Cover: Foto ©Andreas Hilbeck / pixelio.de

More available books at **www.hansebooks.com**

THE

LADY OF WINDERSLEE

A SAINTLY ROMANCE

AND

OTHER POEMS

BY

GEO. W. KETTOMAN.

PEN MAR EDITION
CONTAINING PORTRAIT OF THE AUTHOR AND OTHER
ILLUSTRATIONS.

———

BALTIMORE:
PRESS OF THE FRIEDENWALD CO.
1892.

TO

JOHN W. CABLE, Esq.,

THIS VOLUME IS VERY GRATEFULLY

INSCRIBED BY

THE AUTHOR.

PREFACE.

The LADY OF WINDERSLEE is one of my juvenile works. It may have many faults. It was written by a mountain boy in a wood-chopper's cabin. In explanation of the poem I will say that six years are supposed to have elapsed between the date of the episode mentioned in Idyl I. and that of Idyl III., and some months additional between Idyls III. and IV. In the latter space occurred the death of the mother of our heroine, which seems to have caused a deep melancholy to pervade her nature, once so cheerful, and awaken a sublime spirituality having dealings with prophecy. It should not be supposed that "Calla Land" (declared to have been an ancient *kingdom*) was located just over the "spicy mountains" from the "Vale of Agawan," for I would remind my readers that the body of the work is eminently American in character, so that this "Calla (lily) Land" existed only in the fruitful imagination of the weird singer, who suited the name to the partial ear of the lover of the lilies, to whom, no doubt, his song was specially directed.

It is a notable fact that our Blessed Master from among the thousand flowers of Judea chose the lily to illustrate His gospel to man, complimenting its beauty, thereby giving it a most distinguished place in the history of flowers.

G. W. K.

TRELLISVERDE COTTAGE, NEAR PEN MAR PARK, 1890.

THE LADY OF WINDERSLEE.

RENASCENCY.

Full twenty years have passed away since died sweet Alvia Lee,
The saintliest saint that ever dwelt in happy Winderslee ;
Where now, all through the light of day and night-gloomed shadow deep,
Twelve paces from the chapel-door her sacred ashes sleep.

Still as of old the rain-dove wails above the gusty hill,
And bitterns bugle to the moon by sedgy pool and rill ;
And the round sun goes up and down across the mountains green,
While all the valley lies in light and pleasantness between.

The cry of bleating lambs still comes from glade and meadow gay,
And thin white clouds like bridal veils still fleck the skies of May ;
But yet, with all the bliss I draw from Nature's bounteous store,
The ecstasies that once I knew this valley yields no more.

Full twenty years have passed away since at the even gloam
I took a little hand in mine, in silent paths to roam :
That was the hand of Alvia Lee, the gentle poet-girl,
Among the pure things of this Earth a shining virgin pearl.

We spoke of all the happiness we find in being good,
And much we hear and see of God in forest, field and flood ;
And then we came to talk of death, as what we all must taste,
Before our footsteps can traverse the fair land of the Blest.

I saw a change pervade her face, as when the morning light
Drives happily from a rosy world the heavy-hearted night,
And all the radiance of her soul lit up her starry eyes —
Such being, even then, were fit, methinks, for Paradise !

"Now marvel not," she bravely said, "nor cavil, dearest friend,
Though health and youthful bloom be mine, my life is near its end !
I have so lived that God hath not seen fit to hide the day
When from the thorns and shrines of Earth my soul must go away.

The sign I knew to hearken for, planned in the Heavenly Fold,
(A shepherd calling to a lamb from out the little wold
That shades the mournful churchyard lane), I heard this day at morn,—
Likewise the proof, three moanlike blasts as of a funeral horn !

Assured I am my time is here, and in the slumb'rous night
From out this body lithe and warm my soul must take her flight ;
And when the sweet-eyed Morn reveals the frost on roof and spray,
The tolling bell will throb to tell that I have passed away.

Though 'tis a mystery to me what manner I shall die,
I count it but a little thing, and full of peace am I.
For every pang that I shall feel, ten thousand joys await
When my freed spirit shall have passed the high, white, shining gate !

A parting gift I give you, Claude, to ponder when I'm gone,
Heart-pictures by a lowly hand from beauteous Nature drawn :
Remember me, your changeless friend, when I am with the dead,
When on its last, low pillow lies the simple artist's head !"

Sadly I took the dainty roll, her dear last gift to me,
And through a blinding flood of tears did thank her tenderly.
I cannot tell how much I grieved to think she was to go,
For she was the dearest friend I had in all the long-ago.

We parted. Sleepless passed the night, and lo ! at rise of sun,
Slow tolled the olden chapel bell, its strokes were twenty-one.
To-day I set her portrait in a lily-wreath of gold,
And said, 'Tis mete it should be so for sake of memories old.

Then did I read her soulful songs to those who stood around,
And told them where to find her grave in the mournful churchyard ground ;
And, oh ! I would her name might go to all futurity,
And every age hear of and love the Lady of Winderslee.

Now here I spread her heart's sweet chart and write each melody
Upon the pages of a book for the whole world to see ;
That all possessed of kindly heart may read as well as I,
And know how grand a thing is life when fashioned for the sky.

——the haunted strand,
Where strange historic sculptures and ruins gray with time,
Bleach by a dim white tarn.

IDYL I.

was on a Summer morn, half a dozen years ago,
And the larks were singing sweetly in the daisies'
    scented snow ;
It was jaunty, jolly June, and the sky and earth were
    gay,
When into the flowery dingle we went forth to sport and
    play—
We, the girls of Winderslee—Winderslee, the antique
    town
Founded years and years ago in the vale of Agawan,—
Agawan, *the place of lilies*—AGAWAN, the Indian said,
When he saw the marish flaming with wild lilies golden-red.
With us was the minstrel Claude,—winsome, jolly-hearted youth,
Red his cheeks as any rose, dark his eyes and full of truth.

Brave and beautiful he was, and I own it candidly,
Like a suitor he was loved by each girl in Winderslee.
So he was a rare companion in the rambles of the day,
And we crowned him *"king of love"* with a wreath of laurels gay,
Wrapped we then a chain of daisies 'round and 'round his sweet guitar,
And a wild carnation planted on his bosom like a star.

Like a knight of olden times in a ring of girls he sat,
With the " rosette " on his bosom, and a feather in his hat ;
Then we asked of him a song,—one we ne'er had heard before—
And he answered : You shall hear of the Prince and Alvadore :

Just beyond the spicy mountains, in a vale of Calla Land,
Where a river shadow-freighted ripples over golden sand,
Stand the ruins of a castle all deserted long ago,
And the stone moss and the ivy over all its towers grow.
Chevalier and lady bright tread no more its spacious halls ;
And the crossbow, sword and spear thrill no more against its walls
To the trampled throb of music, for the beautiful and brave
Who once held their revels there long have slept within the grave.

Yea, the hush of death has settled dungeon, court and tower o'er,
Where in all the pomp of splendor dwelt the maiden Alvadore ;
Yet though bred with royal ladies, in the palace of a king,
She was but a peasant maiden—lowly born was she I sing.

The ancient king had brought her from a country far away,
In her rosy babyhood, with his only child to play ;
So the two grew up together, Prince Guindare and Alvadore,
And he loved her as his life,—yea, and even loved her more !
Was she not so pure and sweet that the angels blest the day
She was born into the world in that country far away?

Once, upon a Summer even, in a sweet and quiet place
Where the heliotrope was fragrant, they were standing face to face :
Said he to the fawn-eyed maiden : "I do love you with such love
That the envy of the angels is upon me from above !
Though your spotless heart is mine in the vows you vow to me,
Still the barrier remains and we ne'er can wedded be.
Oh, the iron-handed law ! Dungeons grim and misery !
Take, O maiden, take this token—wear it when I'm dead and gone,
When the cross stands at my grave and the grasses wave thereon."

Saying thus, a crucifix on her trembling heart he laid—
Clasped the chain about her throat. Deep ingravure on it read,
"Farriwell,* aye farriwell." Then a dagger sharp drew he,
Saying in a hollow voice, "In the grave a prince is free !"
Through his heart the dagger passed, and his days were in the yore,
And a voice saying *"Farriwell"* haunts that place forevermore !

When she saw what he had done, poured she all her soul in tears.
"What were life to me," she said, "but a blank of vacant years?
He hath died for love of me whom I cannot live without !"
And in frenzy, lo ! she stooped, plucked the bloody dagger out
From the chamber of his breast—struck it madly through her own,
And the grave of Alvadore and of Prince Guindare are one !

*A quaint form of Farewell.

THE LADY OF WINDERSLEE.

Just beyond the spicy mountains, oft the bards of Calla Land
Chant the mournful story yet, as they pace the haunted strand,
Where strange historic sculptures and ruins gray with time,
Bleach by a dim white tarn dead-hearted but sublime,
And the voice saying *"Farriwell"* echoes up and down a wood,
Where an ancient fountain gurgles like the sound of running blood.

     *   *   *   *   *

It was jolly, jaunty June, half a dozen years ago,
When this tragedy was chanted unto music thrumming low:
I never will forget how the power of the song
In its weird and doleful current floated our young hearts along!
How the strong enchanting minstrel smiled to see us in his thrall,
Having made us drunk with love by a quaint old madrigal!
Not the theme, nor yet the throbbing of the rich guitar in flowers,
But the singer's flaming soul, it was that which melted ours.
Yet I'm sure I do not love in the sense that lovers love:
Mine is only holy *friendship*, like the love of souls above!

IDYL II.

The cardinal lobelia burns along the marshy flume,
And all about the water-mill the pleasant lilies bloom;
The wild rose and the marigold bedeck the grassy slope,
And loco-bells of richest blue a hundred hilltops cope.

The wheat is ripe; the cheery quail is whistling loud and clear;
(I think this is the grandest time of all our Northern year!)
In crimson pride the cherry flames atop the drooping tree,
And many a luscious berry browns adown the sunny lea.
The reaper binds the rustling sheaves against the quivering hill,
And many a scarlet poppy wilts in the oat-fields hot and still.
In fragrant shadows cool and deep the lazy cattle rest,
And the lark in the damp meadow-grass sinks low her speckled breast.

How the sweet myrrh smells hereabout! It grows by this old road:
But how I hate this dragon-mouth, and this bitter-odored woad!
There are even nettles here!—but the myrrh smells out above them all!
So be it with me my whole life—the *sweet* above the *gall*.

Hark how yon merry harvester is shouting at his task !
Now, who could envy him the wine that sparkles in his flask?
Oh, is he not the king of men—the worthiest in the land ?
God bless the sweat upon his brow and the blister on his hand !

I wonder if it would look rude in me to go awhile
Up close to where the reapers are, and watch them at their toil?
Yes : Claude is there where I would go, and he might think it wrong,
So I will tarry where I am and listen to his song.

Hear how he sings of "human love" that "chains a many a heart,"—
I wonder if he's ever felt the sting of Cupid's dart?
Perhaps he has.   He is so kind no maid could treat him ill,
So his would be the flowery side of Love's spice-scented hill.
But bless me ! what is that to me?   Why cling my thoughts to him?
I'll quickly put away from me this query-asking whim :
I'll go and talk with Martha Greene about the birds and flowers,
She has such a very dainty way of dealing with the hours.
And Martha is a darling girl—a joy in any place ;
I'm sure an angel could not have a purer, sweeter face.

I've noticed Claude is fond of her, and doats as much as I
On the rich music of her voice and luster of her eye.
I think she knows it too ! She tries to look her very best
When he's about—and always has a bouquet for his vest.
But—yes, she's very sweet—I always thought her so ;
Claude could do worse than fall in love with Martha Greene, I know.

But what are such affairs to me?   I must not jealous prove ;
Though Claude is very kind to me, I know I'm not in love !
He is my friend—but—well—I'll go and talk with Martha Greene
About the many pleasant things that I this day have seen.

I have not known the flowers so sweet in all my life before ;
The very landscape spreading 'round my raptured eyes adore !
It is not wonderful that Claude has sung the livelong morn,
A brighter day there has not been, I vow, since I was born.
How pipes the sparrow to his mate, and hear the soulful dove :
Oh, this is just a gracious time to sing the songs of love !

IDYL III.

My heart is tangled in a smile and cannot get away !
Till very lately I had thought I'd never see that day.
I feel alarmed, and yet a joy new-born has come to me,
And I might be dissatisfied if I again were free.

Claude says he holds me very dear : I wonder if he does?
They say there are a hundred thorns for every Summer rose !
Why should a fear possess me so? for if I *am* in love,
I still can be true to myself, and true to God above.

I should not dread to be in love ; for love is born of light :
Yet I have heard that love is blind and never sees aright.
How these things be I cannot tell, but Heaven receive the praise,
I trust that grace will follow Claude and me through all our days !

IDYL IV.

I hear the east wind in the pines and in the poplars tall,
And from the damp and misty marsh the rainbird's ghostly call.
The young leaves tremble in the cold, and dismal, seething rain ;
I wish the clouds would break away and sunshine come again !

I sit beside my chamber-hearth and turn my thoughts afloat,
Back o'er the tide of perished years, to sunny isles remote :
I never saw my father's face nor heard his kindly voice ;
They say that he was good and just, and did in God rejoice.
Before my baby eyes beheld the blessed light of day
He met the harpers of the Lord and went with them away !

His Bible in my hands I hold ; my mother gave it me
Before she went to live with him in God's eternity.
I never will forsake this gift, nor wander from its laws ;
I'll take it for a sword and shield in my Redeemer's cause.
The battle is not to the strong, nor to the swift the race,
But to the soul that Jesus Christ in mercy giveth grace.

Since mother's death my heart forlorn lies buried deep in woe.
Sometimes I count it half a sin for me to sorrow so,
But, oh ! I cannot staunch my breast, so wounded to the core,
Nor hope to find again on Earth the generous joys of yore.
My friends are kind ; they pity me, and seek to blunt my grief,
But, oh ! a bruised and mangled heart must break to find relief.

Oh, holy was the boundless love that blest my childhood years,
When in the light of early hope I did not know of tears.
My mother's smile and cheering voice were comforting to me,
And safely up to womanhood they led me pleasantly.
A mother's love, a mother's care, who can repay the debt?
Or when her eyes are closed in death her tenderness forget?

Mine was a mother pure and good : I know her tender eyes
To-day look on the blessed things that are in Paradise !
No more I deck her wavy locks, black as the raven's wing,
With pure white lilies from the flume or from the garden spring ;
But may be in her new bright home do sweeter lilies grow,
And other hands more pure than mine bedeck her angel brow.

She ever loved the lilies best of all the flowers God made,
Because His Son did mention them in His sweet Word, she said :
Likewise because they are so white, so pure and undefiled,
And likened by her gentle heart to the spirit of a child !

I never see a lily bloom without a thought of Heaven,
Or breathing unto God a prayer my sins may be forgiven.
My Saviour, make me pure and white as Thine Own lilies are,
That I may be a bride of Light beyond the morning star !

    *   *   *   *   *

I do remember well the day when in sweet Summertide
Claude asked me share his Earthly lot and be his loving bride.
He asked my hand of mother dear, confessing love for me :
She questioned both to learn our hearts, then said contentedly,
" Dear children, if you love indeed, I cannot say you nay;
Take Jesus for your guide through life, and start upon the way."
We said, " Our mother, you shall be the counselor in our home,
That from the path of rectitude our steps may never roam."
She wept, and said, " The time will come when you would be alone,
Make Christ your guide and He will lead when I am dead and gone."

How little did we think that day, in love's triumphal hour,
That when the early Winter winds should thrill the belfry tower,
We'd lay that dear wise mother down in the cold clay below,
And I go thence an orphan child, blind with the floods of woe!
Thou blessed Christ, thou martyred Lamb, that didest die for me,
Uphold me in my loneliness and keep me close to Thee!

IDYL V.

Over ocean, hill and valley, over wooded slope and plain,
Come the languid airs of Summer, strewing sweetness in their train,
And again the lilies loll under skies of liquid blue,
And I greet them with a sense of pleasure warm and true.

Oh, the lilies are the dearest of the flowers of the vale;
Dearest—for my mother asked me when her cheeks began to pale,
Not to fail to plant them thickly (when she would be out of pain)
On her grave beside the chapel, by the willow-shaded lane.

Yea, and they are blessed flowers which my mother loved so well!
Half the love I have for them human tongue could never tell:
I have moistened them with tears on a dying parent's breast,
And I've pressed them to my bosom where to-day she lies at rest.

Ah, it seems to me sometimes as I gaze on them and cry,
That it would be better with me if I could lie down and die;
For my mother was the dearest, dearest friend I ever knew,
And I know I cannot meet her till the angels call me too—

Till the lilies grow above me as they grow above her now;
Till the clay is on my coffin, and the pallor on my brow;
Till my soul is ushered into the grand eternal Spring,
And her eyes behold the lilies in the garden of my King.

O saintly lily-flowers, when I look from you to Heaven,
And remember Jesus died that my sins might be forgiven,
I cannot suppress the prayer that I soon may rise and go
To the lily-land of God where the blessed are I know.

Few on Earth would mourn, I ween, if I should go hence to-day,
For this world is very cold, and it cares not for my stay.
It can move along without me.   There's but *one* methinks would grieve,
If to-day I should be called, and my spirit take her leave.

But I must not grow so sad, for the world is full of song ;
The lark is with the lily, and the hymn is on her tongue !
And my Lord will know the time that is best for me to go,
Then His gentle voice will call me, and its tones be sweet and low.

IDYL VI.

I walk along the hillside, the sun is shining bright,
And all the vale of Agawan is radiant with light
That fires the thousand windows of olden Winderslee,
The place of my forefathers, a village dear to me.

The lithesome lark is singing amid the reedy bosk,
And flutes the soaring plover in heaven's bosom lost ;
And I hear the dove's soft cooing, neither voice of woe nor joy,—
Intonation of the heart when the thralls of love employ,—
Yet with all this light and music I am filled with restlessness ;
Yea, a melancholy glooms me, bordering on a dull distress,
That calls up tears unbidden, that if sorrow were a sin
I were indeed undone and no crown could I win.

But Jesus looks with pity on the people of His love,
And He taketh them from tears to His own sweet home above ;
There He wreatheth them with smiles, yea, and filleth them with joy,
And provideth perfect peace which hath nevermore alloy.

Oh, I shall soon be there !   I know my stay is brief
Where man is a poor pilgrim and weighted down with grief.
And yet I needs must mourn, for there is one I love
Who may not then go with me to my new home above.
When I am gone, oh, may his feet be never found astray ;
Dear Lord, be gracious unto him and keep him in the way.

Last night as I lay musing supinely on my bed,
I marked a shining halo come circling 'round my head,
And little bursts of music were answering here and there
About my lonely chamber, enchanting the still air.

I knew a Heavenly vision was making way to me,
And calmness filled my bosom, for I desired to see.
Yea, I was quite resigned—I knew that God was near,
For a sense of His good will filled my brave heart with cheer.
I opened wide my eyes that I might discern it all,
The while a death-watch ticked against the hollow wall.
I waited for a time, and then a pure white dove,
(I took it for a symbol of Jesus' precious love,)
Came hovering over me, and nestled on my breast.
I felt a quickening power—was sanctified and blest,
And all my being ran into a flame of love,
That from the altar of my heart burned 'round the brooding dove.

I heard a sound of wings, and after that a voice ;
But know not what it said.   My heart did so rejoice
That understanding fled : but when my sight returned,
An angel clad in white beside me I discerned,
Who made me gracious speech, and said, Behold, I bring
To you a precious lily from the hand of the Great King:
He sends it as a token of His good will and love,
And to assure your bleeding heart there's joy for you above !

She placed in my right hand the flower from Paradise,
And then I thought I saw her go right up into the skies ;
And when I looked where she had stood, behold, she was not there,
But the fragrance of her garments still sweetened all the air.

I peered into the pearl-white bell which trembled in my hand,
And there I read my days are few in this world's barren land.
It was written all in crimson—it looked to me like blood—
And then I thought of Calvary, and said, *My King is good !*

So now I am forewarned.   My Shepherd's voice I'll hear
Before the Winter winds blow cold to close the fleeting year.
O Death, I fear thy agonies ; and yet my faith is strong,
And have not I a promise sweet to bear my steps along?

IDYL VII.

The gum-trees are in scarlet, the maples caped with gold,
And I hear the acorns falling in the little chapel wold ;
The spider looms her web in the weedy stubble-field,
And the cricket chirps secure in brambles thick concealed.
The lonely sparrow frets in the amber-fruited thorn ;
Perhaps she will be far away before another morn :
So flies the soul of man—so leaves she all below
When God's appointed time has come for her to rise and go !

The hills are blue and smoky, the sun is warm and dim,
And burns within a halo—a golden vapor-rim—
That heralds coming storms ; yet such I may not hear,
For I anticipate a change which now is very near.
I'm going to a palmy land where bides eternal Spring,
And Autumn never comes to drive away the birds that sing.
I am assured that I shall go before the snows come down,
Before the pools are frozen and woods and fields are brown.

I shall not hear the ice again crack on the old mill-pond ;
Before the skaters gather there my soul will be beyond !
But may be I will see them through the windows of the sky,
And if I do I'll try to send a blessing from on high.
Yes, I will be in Heaven then, my faith assures me so ;
My body will be sleeping sound at the coming of the snow !

But, gentle Claude, you must not weep, nor wish me back again,
For I shall then be resting sweet and free from every pain.
'Tis true that I myself at first was troubled for your sake,
And the dread thought of leaving you made my whole being quake :
But now I am resigned, and you should be so too ;
Yet 'tis a solemn thing to part when hearts are warm and true.

Think oft of this and don't complain—*God doeth all things well ;*
And then how soon you too must go Himself can only tell.
Lo, if we never parted, Claude, nor breathed the dying sigh,
We'd never know the perfect bliss of meeting in the sky !

Had we both lived another year I would have been your bride,
For to have kept my promise true had been my greatest pride.
I used to think how we would live in the cottage on the hill,
Seeing the waters in the glen turning the old grist mill :
Likewise how you would sing for me at golden gloaming time,
And I read in return some quaint and pleasant rhyme,
Or press a kiss upon your lips and bid you sing again,
And blend my little voice with yours in the familiar strain.

Then, too, I've thought how we would walk along the bloomy hill,
When the silver-jeweled moon were full and the green world were still,
And talk of those we'd love, and those who would love us,
And find in such delightful things an all-absorbing bliss.
Then, when the Winter's fleecy cloak were wrapped about the Earth,
I've thought how love and cheerfulness should smile about our hearth :
And if to glad our humble home, children to us were given,
What joy to mould their tender hearts for righteousness and Heaven !

But these dear things can never, nay, never, never be ;
So let the will of God be done, and do not grieve for me.
I would have been rejoiced, dear Claude, to have become your wife,
And lingered by your side throughout a long and pleasant life :
I know we could have lived as human mates should live,
Nor ever hurt a neighbor's heart, or make a creature grieve :
But God has laid His hand between, and let His will be done,
That we may have a fuller life through His most holy Son.

Oh, let me dry your tears, sweet Claude ; peace cometh by-and-by ;
And you may win another love as fond and true as I.
The world is full of earnest hearts, and everywhere they be,
So you may win a worthier yet than humble Alvia Lee.
Now there is gentle Martha Greene, she has an angel face.
(But yet it is for you to choose if she shall take my place.)
Her heart is just as fond as mine,—and, Claude, you know this too,
She's loved you just as long as I, and doubtless just as true,
But she hides it for my sake. Her cheeks are growing wan—
(O Claude, you must be kind to her when I am dead and gone !)

A many a time I've pitied her, and felt a keen regret
That I was standing in the way her gentle heart was set ;
For she was never envious, but always good and kind,
So next to you I love her best of all I leave behind.

Claude, you have many, many friends, but mine were always few,
So you can spare me better than I could have spared you :
Look up, and see a forming bow in the bosom of the rain,
And all the sunshine of the past may light your path again.

IDYL VIII.

The Country grand and beautiful beyond the rolling sun,—
I thank the Lord its peace is mine when I my course have run ;
Let all the children of the Earth take heart and sing with me
The marvelous love of Jesus Christ, the Lamb of Calvary.

O Holy, Holy, Holy One, so meek, so pure and sweet,
That I could kneel forevermore and kiss Thy blessèd feet !
Oh, wondrous love that cannot fail ! O Christ without compare,
Let all the world look up to Thee with shout, and psalm, and prayer !

Lift up Thy fallen ones, my Lord ; reach down Thy blessed hand
And lead them up the narrow way unto the heavenly land ;
And sing, ye saints, with holy joy that death has lost its sting,
And even Hell must yield her dead to crown Emanuel King !

Our days on Earth are quickly gone, they waste like morning mist
When in the radiant orient it by the sun is kissed ;
But, oh, the heavenly day comes on, which shall forever be,
Nor pain nor death can ever gloom that long eternity.

Love that below is but a germ shall blossom in that day
And yield to God its golden fruit ripe in the mellow ray ;
And all that is of goodly seed to perfect growth shall rise,
That grand and beautiful may be the fields of Paradise.

O Earth, I freely give thee up, thy clouds and ancient sun :
I bless the Lord that I perceive my race is nearly run ;
For I shall wear a crown of light, and be forever blest,
Where daily I may press my head to my Redeemer's breast.

Come, death, with thy pale winding-sheet ; thou hast no terror now ;
Thou bringest but a deeper calm to grace my peaceful brow.
For Christ will waken me ere long to reign with Him on high :—
With faith victorious in my heart submissive I will die.

IDYL IX.

The stars were brightly shining, the moon was over all,
And softly came the sifting of the distant waterfall ;
A lonely cricket chirped beneath my windowsill :
Save these familiar sounds the Autumn night was still.

I looked from out my window, and saw a straying star
Glance down the dark blue heavens, like a bolt of burning spar.
Soon all the sky turned crimson, fierce winds began to roll,
And desolate foreboding passed chilly through my soul !
I saw the stars retiring from out the changing skies,
And then appeared a sweet and beautiful surprise,—
For I had thought the boding was a most evil sign,
And something very bitter in the vision would be mine.

Ah me ! The matchless glory that broke along the skies,
Why did it ever vanish from my delighted eyes ?
It must have been my Lord who walked above the moon,
Whose countenance was brighter than the Summer sun at noon.
I could not look upon Him for the glory of His form ;
Yet was I drawn toward Him, as if by a subtle charm !
White were His flowing robes that trailed a path of light,
And shone with iridescence too luminous for sight.

Ten thousand singing angels triumphant followed near,
Whose lyres of twisted flames mine ears could faintly hear.
And there was one among them, (Oh, well I knew her yet !)
A diadem of jewels was on her forehead set,
And to her sinless bosom there clung a lily-bud—
I saw my own dear mother in her sweet angelhood !

The pageantry moved on with harping, song and light,
And after came the stars, and it again was night.
Long did I heavenward gaze, but the vision grand was gone ;
I prayed for its return, but the stars kept shining on !
Oh, glad am I the day is near when in that blood-washed throng
I'll walk with the redeemed of God and sing the sweet " New Song."

Oh, Hallelujah to the Lord, yea, Hallelujah high !
His children go rejoicing when they are called to die !

IDYL X.

These mournful rhymes will all be Claude's when I am dead and gone ;
Here he can read my thoughts in life while lonely he lives on.
To-day I sing the last, last song which I on earth shall sing—
The murmur of a dying swan that folds her suffering wing !

To-day I take a long last view of upland, vale and rill :
To-morrow Claude will weep alone in his white cot on the hill !
(God pity him, and comfort him, and bless him all his life,
And help him find a path of peace through time's bleak land of strife.)
Methinks I see him worn with grief beneath the boding knell,
Bow down his head in bitter tears for one he lovéd well :
And praised be God that he at least will hold my memory dear,
And consecrate my nameless grave with love's divinest tear !

Poor Alvia Lee, no pompous train will follow her away,
But her frail dust will sleep in Christ the King of kings, for aye.
No lettered pillar rising high will mark her humble grave.
(Nothing but idle grasses there in loneliness may wave !)
But God will know the "unknown spot," (all, all that she need care,)
And send his herald angel down to sound the trumpet there.

My Shepherd's call I heard to-day, at early, early morn,
And afterward the mournful sound as of a funeral horn ;
At midnight when the world is still, and the crescent moon is low,
The angels will demand my soul and she will rise and go—
Leave all the dear old scenes of time for grander things to be—
The scion of a dying stem grafted, my God, in Thee !

Farewell, dear Claude, a fond farewell ! The parting time has come !
Be faithful, and we'll meet again in an Eternal Home.
Now farewell, dear old Winderslee, and each dear thing around,
My feet are going forth to walk my Heavenly Father's ground.
Ah, what could lure me now to stay from Light and Life divine?
O harp, and *crown*, and HOLY ROBE, and JESUS CHRIST, be mine !

FINIS.

THE REQUIEM: IN SEVEN DIRGES.

IN MEMORY OF M. E. K.

CAPUT.

Hard by a woodland wrapped in voiceless gloom
   A troubled bard in speechless sorrow sat ;
He thought upon his child low in the tomb,
   And watched the wheeling of the spectral bat.

Anon a meteor plowed the steel-blue skies,
   And earthward glanced—a slanted lance of spar ;
The peaceful stars beheld with holy eyes,
   And all the winds slept in their caves afar.

Oh, what were life to him who wept unknown
   Of any but the great Omniscient Eye,
Who far from giddy folly mourned a son,
   And smote his breast and heaved the heart-felt sigh ?

In long review came up dear scenes of yore—
   Blessed scenes, which once did fill his heart with joy—
Scenes which Reality can mould no more,
   And Memory but cast in base alloy !

Again he saw the cottage in the glen,
   Hard by a stream that babbles to the wold—
Pictured his dear child's face against the pane,
   Peering to greet his coming as of old !

A hundred paces through the tangled wood
   Where up the brook a narrow footpath wound,
He viewed the schoolhouse by the fenceless road,
   And heard his child shout in the merry round.

Then came the breath of twilights warm and dim,
  In Summers vanished like the early dead,
When to the trembling string rose the rich hymn,
  And on his knee reposed a listening head.

Now rushed the tears, a burning torrent, from his soul,
  Dissolving these rich visions of the heart,
'Till blank Despair resumed her dread control,
  And Frenzy poised her fell, destroying dart.

Then spake a voice from out the pulseless eve,
  And filled the lonely place with music sweet:
"O Bard, it were inhuman not to grieve,
  But put Despair, the viper, 'neath thy feet!

"Awake thy lyre, as erst in happier days
  When thou didst soothe the ear of the sweet dead;
Now Heaven will give to thee sublimer lays,
  And angels weave the laurels for thy head!

"The droning world may fail to heed thy song,
  Some gayer bard may win the praise of men,
But heartfelt notes to angel ears belong,
  And he who wakes them shall not sing in vain.

"Thou shalt have listeners in the wind-blown clouds,
  When like white ships they sail the blue of heaven;
Thy harping shall be heard by unseen crowds
  Where'er by woes thy pilgrim feet are driven!"

Up peered the bard, and, standing at his side,
  An angel smiled into his tear-stained face;
Grander than ever posed terrestrial bride,
  She stood erect in heavenly-moulded grace.

His heart revived as doth the withered rose
  When showers descend on the green world of June;
Now from his harp a new-born music flows,
  And angels keep the solemn strings in tune.

FIRST DIRGE.

Forth from his cot below the sunlit peaks
  Alone the poet roves at morning-tide,
And thus his burdened lyre its silence breaks
  To pitying angels walking at his side :

Thou shalt not moulder in the grave unsung,
  My noble boy ! Though rude the melody,
Rich is the love that stirs its chords among,
  And prompts my heart to sing thy elegy.

In God's own image truly thou wast made—
  A noble child, who had no fear of death—
Whose dying lips said, "I am not afraid."
  How brave thy heart ! how beautiful thy faith !

Hadst thou lived on, my hero-poet boy,
  What wondrous possibilities were thine !
Thy life had been thy wistful father's joy,
  For thy sweet soul was filled with fire divine.

Thou hadst ambition of sublimest sort—
  Courage that might have startled all the world,
And on the highest towers of Fame's great court
  The ensigns of thy victories unfurled.

Thou mightst have won a sepulchre with kings,
  Had warrior-bards extolling 'round thy shrine,
Have won the royal wreath that power brings
  For sculptor's art 'round chiseled brows to twine.

But rather thou hadst craved a nobler tomb,
  One with the martyrs of the "eternal right,"
O'er whom God's flowers are not ashamed to bloom,
  Nor His white stars to pour their holy light.

Thou wouldst have been a hewer staunch and wise
  In the great wilderness of human thought ;
Thy school of logic might have charmed the skies,
  And through thy lips the very angels taught !

Burst, O my soul, thy liquid depths of love,
  And drown thyself in thy own tender tears !
Mourn for the pure—wail for the spotless dove,
  Who doubly died in boyhood's halcyon years !

Fly, O sad spirit, to the hallowed place
  Where he deep sleeps, and grave this tribute there :
Here lies an honor to his God and race ;
  Then turn aside, embrace thy wild despair !

SECOND DIRGE.

Spring decks her cap with daisies and soft ferns,
  And languid lingers on the silken mead ;
From warm South isles the swallow home returns,
  And in lush fields the lambs begin to feed.

A thin mist trails its crystal-bordered veil
  Lightly across the smiling face of morn ;
A tenderness enthralls the landscape pale,
  And out of peace a dreamy rest is born.

There is a quiet in my soul befitting love,
  Yea, and the music of a tender song :
The calm alone constrains the turtle-dove
  To charm the vale with soft, melodious tongue.

This be the solemn subject of each strain—
  The memory of a mournful Autumn scene :
Slowly I see a humble funeral train,
  With winding course go down the hills between.

No famous dust yon doleful hearse doth bear ;
  O'er royal clay no plume nor pennon waves ;
Only a beauteous child rides calmly there,
  Down to the cold, white-pillared land of graves.

No bugle blast affrights the drowsy land ;
  No muffled drum signals the martial tread ;
But, better far, with that meek funeral band
  Walks Jesus Christ, King of the quick and dead !

His little vassal, dearly loved of Him,
　For sin's domains too innocent and sweet,
Goes down to rest in regions still and dim,
　Till Earth her dear restoring Lord shall greet.

Blessed be his sleep till that most righteous God
　He trusted all his days shall call him forth,
A radiant creature from the mouldering sod,
　Restored and glorified through second birth.

Then will he serve his Master dear again,
　Even more fitly than in perished days,
And his grand soul, triumphant over pain,
　Embrace the never-ending life of praise.

THIRD DIRGE.

Now Summer brings the harvest-time once more,
　And golden waves flame up the wheated hills ;
The sickler gathers in the precious store—
　The store of bread our gracious Father wills.

But he I mourn views not this cheerful scene ;
　Unconscious he of harvest jubilee ;
He cannot see the forests draped in green,
　Nor lilies loll along the tufted lea.

Unknown of him by marsh and rushy flume
　The cardinal lobelia swings her torch ;
Alike unknown the rockbell tolls her bloom,
　And in brown swaths the luckless poppies scorch.

The Summer cloud, white as a bridal veil,
　That slowly drifts across the tender blue
He seeth not, nor hears the plaintive wail
　Of soulful winds that drink the morning dew.

High in the middle air the plover flutes
　His dirge of sighs in long-drawn notes and wild ;
Such music weird my sombre spirit suits—
　Turns all my being to my perished child !

'Twas yester-eve, when gloomed the twilight grey,
　I poised on yonder cliff to think of him :
In the warm West a glorious vision lay,
　And strange cloud-figures decked the world's vague rim.

Lo, phantom forms in burning armor clad
　Manned red triremes sliding on saffron seas :
I had a dream of spirits brave and glad
　Guarding the outer coasts of Paradise !

And far beyond I seemed to see the goal—
　The Holy Port in silvery, silken light !
I felt a rapture gathering in my soul :
　I said, The Lord will comfort me this night.

A goodly psalm began to move my tongue,—
　Perhaps the angels worded it for me ;
Solemn and stately rose the hallowed song,
　For there were singers that I could not see :

Oh, holy, holy is the name of God,
　Whose mighty hand the Earth's foundations laid.
Though million worlds are by His glory awed,
　The Lord will not forget His faithful dead.

The boundless universe He rules with power
　And justice, for it all by Him was made,
And though a century with Him is as an hour,
　The Lord will not forget His faithful dead.

A sparrow falleth not without His note,
　Unseen by Him no flower its bloom doth spread,
Nor even rain-born bubbles rise and float—
　The Lord will not forget His faithful dead.

In crypt, in mausoleum, mound or grave,
　Marked or unmarked, their last low silent bed,
The Lord doth know His people and will save,—
　Yea, He will not forget His faithful dead.

Shout, O creation, to His hallowed fame !
Let all things formed adore their sacred Head,
Crying, Holy, holy, holy is God's name :
His promise shall restore the faithful dead !

FOURTH DIRGE.

Pale Autumn, robed in yellow for her woes,
Spatters the forests with the hue of blood ;
And after her the strong wind whirls and blows,
And rasps the stained leaves from each groaning wood.

The rose is dead upon my darling's grave ;
The stricken grasses writhe above his breast :
Woe, woe is me ! Sorrow, behold thy slave !
Sweet son, I would I were like thee—at rest.

My dear dead boy, once so divinely fair,
How can I e'er forget thy merry voice?
Thy rosy face and lustrous golden hair,
And thy sweet eyes—they make me still rejoice !

I sing the songs that used to please thee well,
When all alone I pace yon friendly wold,
Wrapped in the sweets of memory's magic spell,
And with each strain comes back some joy of old.

I say sweet things I heard thee say in life :
I call thy name—no answer comes to me :
Tears flow again : I clasp my hands in grief
And moan aloud to think it thus must be.

But who can change the hidden plans of God ?
Or move the tomb to yield its blessed dead ?
Can human tears roll back the growing sod,
Or woo to Earth the soul forever fled?

FIFTH DIRGE.

See Winter like a pale ghost scale yon peak,
  And trail his mantle far adown the vale ;
In ice-walled cells imprisoned runnels shriek,
  And hoar-frost sparkles in the sheltered dale.

Shrill pipes the spectral blast about the cliff,
  And hollow moaning enters every cave,
As if he seeks the very soul of grief,
  To woo her forth, with him to whine and rave.

The owl sits in barred feathers to his ears
  Brooding on desolation and thick gloom,
Fit emblem of the spirit of the years
  That sees each living thing approach a tomb !

Cloud-temples built by vapory architects,
  And gleaming rockeries of crystal light,
Float hurriedly o'er heaven's blue index,
  On wind-rafts drifting to the world of white.

Now steps a priestess down a porphyry stair,
  Clad in clear samite, decked for minstrelsy,
From some kind temple in the middle air
  Sent forth to soothe the throes of misery.

She strikes her harp of mellow flames enwrought,
  And hear the song that floods the frosty day :
Peace, *peace!* Hath not high-priced the Shepherd bought
  His sheep? Thy lamb, sweet lamb, shall see the May !

Vex not thy mind with bodings of despair—
  With wintry thoughts that freeze the very soul :
Peace—come away ! Beyond the Winter drear
  Sweet streams must through eternal verdure roll !

Uprear the shelter—Faith. He only sleeps,
  And when the morning cometh he shall wake,
Wake even when the first red dawn-ray leaps,
  And angels sing for very gladness' sake.

Dost dream this life holds all there is of man?
Canst thou not feel the *soul* within thyself
Throb at the clearness of the Divine plan?
And is man satisfied with food and pelf?

Ah, no—else why the subtle fear of doom
Sown all along the pathway of this life?
Lay hold on truth! Gaze hopefully on the tomb:
It is the soul's escape from Earthly strife.

A little while and thou shalt be as he—
The snow will pile above thy quiet rest;
The wind will shake the tombstone over thee
And weirdly moan above thy mouldering breast.

The toad may make her nest within thy skull,
And the numb snake lie coiled among thy bones;
Of foul green mould thy coffin may be full,
And ghouls gnaw at the lid with shrieks and moans!

But what of that? Unknowing thou shalt sleep;
A little space, and thou shalt live again,
To see the soft mists cap the vernal steep,
And white flocks cluster on the musky plain.

Yea, thou mayst walk among the glorified,
In long converse with him thou mournest now:
What matter then that once ye both were dead,
Seeing eternal life warm on each brow?

Come, come away, and leave him to his rest;
Tears, bitter tears can never better him,
But weaken thee and blur God's high behest—
Deep sap the mind, and make faith's vision dim.

Beware of dreamers!—*keep the olden faith,*
For science is a suckling on the Earth,
That much self-wise about creation brayeth,
Yet cannot give one puny insect birth!

Nor be thou all unmindful of the dead :
  Thou art a sire : dead is thine only son :
'Tis proper that the tears of love be shed,
  But in thy sorrow be not thou undone.

The Winter's storm shall perish from the wold,
  And ice-bound streams laugh in the sunny ray :
Lo, Heavenly warmth shall thaw the Earthly cold,
  And Christ bring in a never-ending May.

SIXTH DIRGE.

Proof undeniable of the eternal life,
  Deep-rooted, props man's frail, distrustful soul,
And with the legend doubts makes vengeful strife
  Though atheistic Hell's vague thunders roll.

The grave's long night at last must wither gray,
  And life's effulgent morn crimson again ;
Man, the divine, shall know eternal day,
  Through Christ victorious over death to reign.

When that great morn shall rouse the millions dead,
  Oh, may I see my child, my own once more,
With radiant crown encircling his fair head,
  With God's elect walking the Heavenly shore.

Then my glad heart may wholly understand
  Things that now make my blinded spirit weep :
Oh, there can be no mystery in that land,
  And no red grave vaulting a doleful sleep !

Though Hell should be my poor soul's final doom,
  Yet if I may but know my little son
Hath part in Heaven's deathless joy and bloom,
  I'll bless the Christ until my strength be gone !

I can but weep. O Master, pity me !
  Give me, I pray, sweet faith to make me strong ;
Reach down Thy hand and hold me close to Thee,
  Lest in my anxious fervor I go wrong.

SEVENTH DIRGE.

This is no dream.   It must be death indeed!
Yon glimmering window dwindles to a spark,
And whirling dulls to gray—swims my numb head,
    And voices muffle in the growing dark!

I'm going—up, up, up!—oh, let me go!
    God bless the stricken ones I leave behind—
Farewell—let the white roses bud and blow—
    Let the cold marbles tremble in the wind!

Halleluiah—Halleluiah—comes the change!
    Light, blessed light! no death at last!   The dawn
Of some great day spreads round me soft and strange—
    All my sweet DEAD henceforth shall be my own!

Ring, golden harp, ring wild and wonderful
    Across green plains, across the Jasper Sea!
Redeemed at last!   O ever-singing soul,
    Through Jesus Christ thou hast thy victory!

POEMS.

A DREAM OF FAME.

" The truth of dreams is their reverse."—ANON.

Leander, toiler on his native hills,
One Summer day did lean him to an oak,
To slack the sinews of his aching arms,
And while he stood, a vision came to him
And wrapped him in its luring labyrinths :

Behold, a sunny-headed mountain boy,
Afar off heard the lusty cry of Fame,
Loud piping on her gnarléd shell the praise
Of men whose bones had sodden for
A thousand years in myrtle-covered tombs,
With deep-carved stones uplifted to the gaze
Of passing man. Ah, poor, ambitious boy,
He sighed for such a lot, nor counted odds !
The axe, his friend in all his former days,
Became a loathsome serpent in his hand ;
He longed to strive among the mighty minds
That mould the destiny of nations, or
Refine the crude and lawless passions of
The human race, or soothe them into peace
With the full powers of minstrelsy divine.
The latter longing him possessed, and lo !
The mild Muse of his native woods appeared,
In rustic mantle clad, and laurel'd locks,
Smiled on her new-found lover, and did place
Within his hand her own wild harp. He wept
For joy, and struck the brazen wires until
The hollow void around discordant jarred
With harsh vibrations, dinsome to the ear.

Emboldened at his sad lack of skill,
Despair at first made conflict with his hopes,
But, learning of the lark and sparrow fond,
He made his lays partake of melody,
And sweeten as the listless days sped by.
At last on sunny Summer morns, behold
The people came, and clustered 'neath the oaks,
To hear his songs, and praise him for his skill.

Leander knew the picture of himself ;
Toiled for the wreath of Fame and—died obscure !

TESSIE.

A letter from Tessie,
        What a treat !
For Tessie's the essence
        Of all that's sweet.
Tessie's the whole round world to me,
And more than this she cannot be :
Even if she were my sweet wife,
She couldn't be closer to my life.

A letter from Tessie,
        Brother mine ?
A letter from Tessie
        Is quite divine.
She writes so fair and round a hand,
And has of language such command,
That whether we be friend or lover,
We read the sweet page over and over.

A letter from Tessie,
        Bless my soul !
Let me kiss and open the dear, dear scroll.
I know 'tis filled with the sweetest things,
Gathered where Fancy plumes her wings :
As I break the crimson seal so neat,
The attar of roses rises sweet.

A letter from Tessie,
  A portrait too !
O the exquisite pleasure ! —
  What shall I do?
I'll go and pray for the little dear,
That she may cheer me many a year ;
And this sweet face shall stay with me
Till I go down where the still hearts be !

TERSABEL.

  Tersabel,
  Tersabel,
For my life I could not tell
If you love me ill or well :
 You are full of mystery ;
Never saying what you mean,
Never meaning what you say ;
Posing oft in tempting way,
Always keeping me at bay :
O you cruel fairy queen,
Tell me, tell me what you mean—
 Cast away the mystery.

  Tersabel,
  Tersabel,
Are you kind, or are you haughty ?
Are you good, or are you naughty,
 Roguish, romping Tersabel ?
Are you true, or are you false ?
Or the victim of impulse ?
Are you silly ? Are you wise ?
Or a witch in sweet disguise,
Sent to torture me a season,
 And dethrone my boyish reason ?
Oh, I wish that I could tell
What your purpose, Tersabel !

When I press an honest suit,
  Then you spring up from your seat,
And you speak of bitter fruit
  Growing from a blossom sweet!
O you dull interpreter!
  I don't want to lead you in
  The deceptive paths of sin,
Scented with the smell of myrrh!
  Love if true is *purity*,
  And our best security.

When a little I am silent,
  And refuse to talk of love,
Then you taunt me with caresses,
Ay, and smother me with kisses,
Mingled with suspicious sighs,
And a languor of the eyes
  That makes my sluggish pulses move.
Then when I am found excited
You seem suddenly delighted—
Run away and laugh at me,
Pressing both your sides in glee;
And you will not let me kiss you,
Nor allow me to caress you,
Even will not let me tell
How I love you, Tersabel.

You are cruel, Tersabel
  Thus to tease a lover kind;
  Thus to keep him ever blind
  To the intent of your mind;
  And if he should courage find
To approach you, Tersabel,
  Thus to mock him and declare
  You have reason to take care!

Tell me what you mean, my dear?
  Do you keep me for a toy?
Things sometimes look mighty queer—
  Am I not a silly boy
  Thus to suffer day by day
  And refuse to stay away?

Pardon, pardon, Tersabel!
Do you love me ill or well?
Throw your laughing robe aside—
Will you ever be my bride?
Very well,
Tersabel!
Pinch your sides and laugh at me—
Very shortly I shall see
What you mean by teasing me!

STUDYING THE BUST OF MILTIADES.

NOTE.—Miltiades was a celebrated Greek general, and the same who defeated a powerful Persian army on the plains of Marathon with a handful of Athenians, in about the year 490 B. C.

Ah, what a face! Methinks the eternal gods
Did fashion it from Jupiter's. Observe the eye:
It seems a pit of fire, the mightiest floods
Might never quench, though water rose from earth to sky!

The brows are hung like thunder-clouds above
The orbs of vision: lo, the nose betrays
A tiger's back! The widespread nostrils hove
Like panting bellows strained to fan Hell's keenest blaze!

Proudly the flame-like beard rolls from the mouth,
And adder-tongued doth lick the cold breastplate,
Well wrought of thick steel scales. 'Twere worth
A world, like he, to *scorn*, *defy* and CHALLENGE Fate.

The hair is like a full-grown lion's mane
Under the helmet; and the shoulders mock
At common strength. The massy forehead's frame
Is like a furrowed wall, or like a time-plowed rock.

Yet in this strong majestic face are blent
Virtues the mighty even can exalt:
I see the *patriot*, the *martyr*, and the *saint*—
The lily here is twisted with the thunderbolt!

THE BELL AT MONTEREY.

Written on hearing the bell of Hawley Memorial Chapel ringing on a
Summer evening.

NOTE.—The Hawley Memorial Chapel is located at Monterey, Pa., and
was erected by a Baltimore lady in memory of her husband, the late Martin Hawley, Esq. As soon as it was completed the generous lady opened
its doors to the surrounding community as a place of public worship.

Beyond where Mount Dunlap in pride
 Lifts high his emerald-turban'd head
The warm-eyed sun had swooned and died,
 And all the wild West wept in red.

When, standing on a breezy steep,
 I heard the bell at Monterey ;
My heart sprang in a sudden leap,
 And thus you might have heard me say :

The virtuous die nor are forgot,
 (God loves the graves that hold their dust),
They die, but lo ! they perish not,
 Because in God they have their trust.

Ring sweetly *in memoriam,*
 Bell of the hills, thy call to prayer,
And gospel voice, and sacred psalm :
 Ring out thy mission rich and rare.

Sweet mountain bell, o'er scar and fell
 I hear thy silvery echoes roll ;
Ring on, rouse every hill and dell,
 Call to the very farthest soul !

God hath a mission for us all
 While in the feeble flesh we dwell ;
It may be great, it may be small,
 But bless'd are they who fill it well.

The only passport to the skies
 Is love of God and fellow-man,
With works of faith and sacrifice,
 According with Jehovah's plan.

Ring out, sweet bell, thy call sublime ;
Ring in the erring soul from far ;
Ring till the angels hear the chime,
And set the gates of Heaven ajar.

Long may thy ample pæan tell
Of Jesus and redeeming love,
And all who hear it, O sweet bell !
Find fellowship with Christ above.

Thou art become my *angelus*,
And at thy sound I bare my head
And pray, Be merciful to us,
Thou Jesus risen from the dead.

Ay, ever be my *angelus*,
And sacred meditation bring,
Until I hear the bells of Peace
On Zion's Holy Mountain ring.

Thanks to the good and generous heart
That brought thee to our land of hills,
To woo our people to depart
From sin and its ten thousand ills.

The virtuous die nor are forgot,
(God loves the graves that hold their dust),
They die, but lo ! they perish not,
Because in God they have their trust.*

TO AN EAGLE.

ON SEEING IT PERCHED ON THE OBSERVATORY, HIGH ROCK.†

Why cam'st thou, grey old eagle, here?
Art thou a token, or a seer?
Or wast thou cyried in this ledge,
And, having flown at the presage

* The above lines were written at suggestion of Mr. Francis T. King,
and were read by him at the anniversary of the dedication of the Chapel,
Sunday, August 10th, 1890.

†A famous point on the Blue Ridge Mountains, on the western border of
Maryland, visited annually by not less than 125,000 people.

Of crafty man's approach, art come
To view once more thy fledgling home ;
Haply to close thy fading eye
In the place of thy nativity?

Change here hath wrought since thou wert young,
When thy mother's voice all fearless rung
From cliff to cliff, and peak to peak,
Far answered by the panther's shriek,
Untrammel'd liberty's address
To an unbroken wilderness.
Bold man hath here assayed to rear
A riot-castle for his cheer,
And brought his gentler mate to stand
On these borders sweet of Aeriel's land,—
Not satisfied with upward show,
Here climbed the heavens to look below !

Oh, lov'st thou still those dark-green pines,
Bristling along the windy spines
Of mountains stretching through the sky,
A witching scene to every eye?
And lov'st thou yet yon nether view
Of meadows tinged with tender blue,
Whose streams are gliding soft and slow,
Thousands of feet thy perch below?
And dost revere these ancient rocks
That scorn the tempest's mightiest shocks ;
That mirthful toy, when storms are near,
With the hot lightning's lurid spear,
And echo-mock the grim gust king,
Fierce riding on Plutonian wing,
Piercing the earth at every vein
With the cold arrows of the rain?

O fearless bird of cloud and sun,
Nurtured upon the thunder's throne !
Like thee, I too admire this place,
Adorned with every rural grace.

The poet's and the eagle's heart,
Have sympathies not much apart :
The same strong love of liberty ;
Ear swift to hear and eye to see,
And flash of spirit quick and far,
Like lurid gleam of falling star ;
The same respect for solitude,
Sublimity of peak and flood ;
The same unwavering love of home,
Where'er the wandering footsteps roam ;
The same desire Heavenward to rise,
A living meteor up the skies.

I cannot tell what thoughts are thine
While lingering here, but these are mine :
Here *Magnitude* declares how great
The power of Heaven's high potentate,
And shows conceited creature man
A pigmy vile in Nature's plan,
And grey *Antiquity* appears,
And speaks of long-forgotten years,
Ages engulfed in numbers vast
In the dark chasm of the past.
Here *Law* and *Order* sit and smile
On kind *Obedience* all the while,
And *Change* toils on with steady hand,
Nor swerves from Heaven's fixed command
To grind the mighty rocks to sand.
Here *Beauty*, like a roving child,
Comes scattering sweets through all the wild,
And *elfin minstrels* bugle sweet
Where the wind-enamored pine-boughs meet,
Atop this minaret of the world,
Where cool, refreshing clouds are curled,
To run aslant the green-rimmed earth,
And give a wider beauty birth.
Hail sense of *prayer*, hail POWER'S ROD,
Hail presence of the living GOD !

CORPORAL JOHN.

Beyond the town of Gettysburg, in Fame's immortal scene,
Still stands the cot of Corporal John, hard by a woodland green ;
And farther down the hollow, friends, it would be sweet employ
To show you where his bones are laid beside his little boy.

And now I have a tale to tell.   It hath its bitter sin ;
But you would scarcely care to hear if the evil were not in.
A farmer's son was Corporal John, in times that used to be,
And, following his father's plow, a natural prince was he.
And Nature in her plan decreed that there should rise a queen,
To claim and rule his noble heart and modify the scene ;
So Mary Bell, the miller's child, royal in maiden charms,
Drank with him of the cup of love and owned his sheltering arms.

Two years they lived in wedded bliss, and pure and undefiled,
Unto her princely husband-boy sweet Mary bore a child ;
But ere his little feet could walk across the cottage floor,
One day a dashing cavalier came riding by the door.
He saw the happy mother there, for Summer gaily dressed,
The laughing baby at her feet, a wild rose on her breast.

He dropped a careless courtesy, and she returned the same,
Surely not guessing Time would mark therein the seed of shame,
But every day of that whole week that man came riding by,
And every time to Mary sweet he dropped a courtesy.
Now Mary came to wonder much the stately stranger's name,
And asked her husband John one day if he could tell the same.

" Yes, Mary dear," he made reply, " they call him Captain Horr ;
His business is recruiting men for service in the war.
He'll call here in a day or two to get my ' yes ' or ' no ' ;
He claims I look so soldierly, he'd like to have me so,
And even says that I may win renown and honors grand,
And hopes you'll not object to have me serve our native land."

The Captain called and, smooth of tongue, soon won the wife's consent,
And down into the sulphurous South the " new recruit " was sent,
But still the Captain rode that way and, seeing Mary grieve,
Paused every day with cheering words her bodings to relieve.

He brought her letters from the town through all the Autumn gay,
And strove to show his sympathy in many a pleasant way.
At last the girl grew kind to him, and joyed to see him come,
Because he brought such hope and joy into her lonely home.
The neighbors 'round were all alert, and slanders took the wind
(All this I can assure you was before the woman sinned),
They turned her down on every side, and even in the church,
Instead of admonition kind they pressed her in the lurch.

Now John was far down in the front, she heard no more from him,
And deep within poor Mary's heart the love of life grew dim.
They saw her running into want for clothing and for food,
And wives forbade their husbands e'en to give the woman wood.
Discouraged, Mary closer clung, as I need scarcely tell,
To him, the demon in disguise, who set her face for hell.

He gave her clothes and jewels fine, he raised her out of want,
And made her cottage by the wood a cosy pleasure-haunt.
Then Mary fell the villain's prey—so falls the lily pale
When crushed against the garden-wall by some ungenerous gale.
Full soon without one pitying sigh the vile wretch fled her bower,
As flies the honey-glutted bee from out the ravished flower.
He went—she never heard again from that deceitful man,
And then the more than dreadful woe of Mary's life began.

Her baby-boy grew pale and drooped, nor could the warm Spring save ;
So Summer blued the violets above his little grave.
These are the last words that he said : " Mamma, I see a star—
Tell papa I have gone to sleep when he comes from the war."

" Papa !" that word from sinless lips broke that frail woman's heart,
And hurled into her quivering breast Remorse's dreadful dart.
Trembling she laid her little boy below the thicket wild,
And mourned with all a mother's love her poor dishonored child.
Through tears another came to her, the offspring of her shame,
But only mocked the void for him who bore her husband's name.

*   *   *   *   *   *   *   *   *   *

Up to our Northern wheat-lands came the great invader Lee,
With ninety thousand men—the boast of Southern chivalry ;

But Heaven decreed he should not go beyond a given spot,
And his defeat at Gettysburg will never be forgot.
Hail to our sixty thousand brave, that grand victorious band,
Whose honor is the heritage and glory of our land !

Among the great defenders there, with iron nerve and will,
Was one whom they called Corporal John, the "Tiger of Chancellorsville."
The soldiers cheered him everywhere as the bloody hours wore on,
For many a sturdy foe went down by the hand of Corporal John.
At last a bullet pierced his breast, he fell to fight no more,
And as they bore him to the rear his comrades wept full sore.

"Benny," he said to one of them, "I hope—I think—don't you,
That I can live a little while—maybe an hour or two?
I'm not so very far from home—raise my head till I see—
My sight is bad—but over there—right past that old oak-tree—
You see that woods across the hill? Your eyes are good—look close—
Down at the lower edge of that, I think I see the house.

"Put me behind this old stone fence, where I won't be trampled on,
And go and fight—don't stop for me—till the bloody task is done.
Then if I should be living yet, and you are living too,
Please take me home, or tell my wife—I'd do the same for you—
God bless her and my baby-boy — if them no more I see,
A thousand blessings on them both—you'll tell them this for me?

"Look in my pocket, you will find a little Bible there—
'Twas Mary's parting gift to me—I've kept it clean with care.
I fear it's staining with my blood—look carefully and see—
I'd like to save it for my child, if that could only be.
'Not stained so much?'—then give it me—yes—put it in my hand,
And now go back and, hero-like, defend our suffering land."

But only two went back to fight ; one watched the dying man,
And one to tell the hero's wife with speed vehement ran,
And paused he not for guard or sneer, but dauntless he rushed on
Till he found his comrade's mate and told the fate of Corporal John.

She gave a shriek of wild despair, her face grew deathly white ;
She clasped her baby in her arms and sped with all her might

Across the hollow and the hill (so speeds a stricken hind),
And wondering soldiers watched her hair stream bronzen in the wind.
The cannons belched their thunder-peals, the screaming shells flew 'round,
But on came Mary and her child across that dangerous ground.
But when she reached her hero's side, his face was chill and pale,
For death with more than charity had drawn the kindly veil.
A smile still lingered on his face (it seemed a heavenly ray),
And in his soft relaxing hand the cherished Bible lay.

*　　*　　*　　*　　*　　*　　*　　*　　*　　*

Now seeking pardon for the past, in her affliction sore,
The lonely wife of Corporal John lives on to sin no more.

VITURIA AND JULIAN.

Before the Roman populace
　　The good Vituria stood ;
Fierce in their cage the lions roared,
　　And panted for her blood,
While with a white uplifted hand
　　Her funeral prayer she poured :

" Forgive my murderers, Jesu kind,
　　Thou who art Lord of all :
They hate me for Thy dear name's sake,
　　And for my blood do call ;
But pity them, for they are weak
　　And blind through Adam's fall.

" Let not Thy wrath abide upon
　　Mistaken, lovely Rome—
Rome, that my fathers died to save—
　　Rome, still my people's home—
Rome, that I bless with my last breath,
　　But has for me no tomb ! "

Then up rose stately Julian,
　And tears suffused his eyes.
" Unloose the woman's chains," he said,
　" High Jove hath heard her cries !
She is a Roman patriot,
　Worthy a victor's prize.

" Bring her to me, my lictors true,
　Most gracious she hath prayed ;
I would not for the gods' fair name
　That such to beasts were fed :
Nay, rather should the *laurel leaf*
　Bedeck her fair young head.

" Father of mercy, mighty Jove,
　Whose thunders jar the sea,
Spare when thy day of vengeance comes
　This friend of Italy :
Though of the *Galilean school*,
　Her virtues are of thee."

Out cried the maid with streaming eyes :
　" O Jesu, bless for me
The gracious Emperor Julian,
　Belov'd of Italy :
Although his prayers ascend to Jove,
　His virtues are of Thee."

O'er all the amphitheatre
　An ominous silence fell,
Till out spoke wise Libanius,
　" ' Tis strange, but it is well ;
And nowhere but in pious Rome
　Hath such a thing befell ! "

THE TRAGEDY.

Two people walked out from Waldamar,
　Through the cedar wood under the hill ;
They passed the grot where the King was stabbed,
　And the flume of the haunted mill.

They paused in the road where the moon shone full—
Solemn, and round, and lone ;
An ominous gleam ran back and forth,
And a woman was heard to moan ;
A ribbon of light slung into a loop,
And the groans of a dying man
Rolled heavily into the cedar wood,
Then the forest was still again.

At morn a traveler passed that way,
Going up to Waldamar ;
The dawn's red fire was burning the wood,
And melting the morning star.
He saw in the road a dismal sight—
A knife, and twain dead there—
A tall young man with a noble face,
And a lady exceedingly fair.
He hurried on to the quaint old town
With its steeples as white as spar,
And told the dreadful sight he saw
To the people of Waldamar.

WASHINGTON'S PSALM.

The air was still 'round Valley Forge, the winter moon shone bright,
And richly from her crescent cup spilled out her silvery light,
Till all the snow-enameled hills swam in a glittering glow,
Like pearls set in the web of light that wrapped the vale below.
The jewels of the Lord—bright stars—burned in the azure dome,
And many a sufferer in their light prayed for the loved at home.
The drifted snow lay cold and deep all 'round the dismal camp,
Betraying with a chilly screech the shivering pickets' tramp.
Soldiers half-clad had built a fire just where the cart-roads crossed,
And high into the thin cold air the twisted flames were tossed ;
And there, belike a tower of hope touched by a rising sun,
Among the men he dearly loved stood fearless Washington :
And suddenly, as if he saw into the times afar,
Or read his country's future state depicted in a star,
He broke into this cheerful psalm, triumphant o'er despair,
And it was sung for many a day by every hero there :

Jehovah, Thou Almighty God,
That rulest the creation broad,
That wrought the chariot of the sun,
And bade the stars their courses run.

This night we glorify Thy name,
Nor sigh for riches nor for fame,
But happy are that we may be
In times to come a people free.

We see the glad years coming up—
Our children sip the golden cup ;
The wine of happiness flows red,
And all the land is full of bread.

The broken chains of Tyranny
Are dragged back through the surging sea,
And Liberty reigns evermore,
Triumphant o'er Columbia's shore.

About our friendly ports arise
The masts of mighty argosies,
With gems from every land to deck
Mild-eyed Fredomia's virgin neck.

And in return, lo ! we behold
Her doling corn, and wine, and gold,
And blessing all with shadowing hands,
The patron of a hundred lands.

O God Almighty, only King,
Let Earth and Heaven Thy praises sing ;
The lowest serf that trusts in Thee
May taste at last of liberty.

Thine arm shall break the yoke of kings ;
Where now the clash of conflict rings,
The seed of love shall yield increase,
And Christ begin His reign of peace.

All men shall learn to reverence good,
And share an equal brotherhood ;
The sons of kings shall reap and mow,
And all their daughters spin and sew.

When that sweet day shall pour its light
O'er continent and island bright,
A deathless song of liberty
From earth shall swell, great God, to Thee.

SPLINTERS OF RHYME,

PLUCKED FROM VARIOUS POEMS TOO LONG FOR
PUBLICATION IN THIS LITTLE BOOK.

INSULTED.

She heard my vows with cold disdain ;
  My heart flew out of tune,
And Love went up to rock himself
  In the bow of the two-horned moon.
Well done, you little elf, said I,
  And when I call you down
For her again, the sun will blaze
  In midnight's starry crown.

POETRY.

O Poesy, thou sunny nymph,
  Sweet feeder of man's hope in God,
(That hallowéd and holy fire
  That warms this chilly funeral road),
To thee I turn in doubt's dread hour,
  Through thee I think I see the Lord,
And trustfully follow on alert
  To hear the unmistaken Word.

A NIGHT PSALM.

While angels spangled the milky-way
With sparks from the brand of immortal day,
  The poet is singing a psalm.
He liveth in love with the works of God,
And, feasting on beauty, he walketh abroad,
  Adoring the mighty "I Am."

Lo, God is the builder of all things fair,
The maker and ruler of sea and air,
   And the author of life and love ;
Now, since He hath fashioned our Earth so grand,
What beauty must hallow His own sweet land,
   And temple, and palace above !

THE THUNDERBOLT.

Livid,
Vivid
Bar of fire,
Flashing,
Crashing
In thine ire
Through the iron-colored clouds,
With the sound of splitting steel,
Making all the hilltops reel,
And the dead shake in their shrouds,
God hath flung thee from His hand
As I toss this grain of sand.

THE WEIR-KING.

In the cloud-mountains of the central air,
  O'er the abysmal chasm of the storms,
  Where writhe the snaky-limbed contorturous forms
Of furies yelling in the frenzy of despair,
  I have my castle, by the purple mists
  And fluffy vapors rimming mighty wastes
Of hollow nothingness thin-breath'd and rare.

MORNING.

On merry toes gay Morning comes
  Through orient beds of pinks,
And every feathered minstrel now
  Her sweet, small lyre clinks.

And everywhere the Master's praise
Flows free in grateful strain;
But oh for that Morn long foretold
When He shall come to reign.

Then shall a grander music rise,
And ring from sphere to sphere:
Oh for a harp of heavenly tone
When I that chorus hear!

FROM THE "FIRE-DAGGER."

A mile at sea the haunted isle
Crouched cowering in the stagnant night;
Dank vapors, rolling pile on pile,
Shut out the salt-white cliffs from sight.

From out the dun mist's purple rim
I saw the dread phantasm leap—
A hand and blade of blood-red flame
That seethed the bosom of the deep.

Grim at my side the bearded king
Sat muttering curses grave and slow;
The shadow of a demon's wing
Fell weirdly on the tide below!

THE TWIN-GABLED COTTAGE.

Beyond the heavy-foliaged wood it stands,
Twin-gabled, looking to the west—red-roofed,
And spurting tall white chimneys through the copse
That grows up higher than its eves, hiding
Its spacious porch, trellised and vined,
As if to shield it from the dusty highway, and .
Repel the quivering heat of brazen noon.

I've passed that sweet place twenty times a month,
And every time beheld a vision rare—
The cotter's daughter, rich in stateliness,
Bland smiles, red cheeks, and soft pink Swiss—
Enough to wound a bolder heart than mine.

I would I were the royal dahlia plant
That charms her sight, and sometimes thrills
At the light touch of her caressing fingers.
But rather would I be her *lover!* Up,
Faint heart ! the coward wins few victories,
And these were better lost than won.

ON THE SHORE.

With joyous scream the seabird skims
    Across the wave-Alps of the sea,
Whose avalanches of cold foam
    Slide down continually.
I gaze with something in my heart
    Held from the wreck of perished years ;
Oh, purer is this priceless gem,
    Since washed with copious tears.

SIMPLE FAITH.

There are some things in God's dear Word I cannot see aright,
But He will some time flood them all with unmistaken light.
Enough I know to find the way—to choose whate'er is good,
And realize my future life was bought with Jesus' blood.
Almighty Father, thanks to Thee that these sweet things I know :
Oh shield this simple faith from doubt while I sojourn below.

BEAUTY.

A FRAGMENT.

Wherever there is *Beauty* there is *Good* :
Though it be latent, it will shoot the bud,
If nourished by congenial sun and showers,
And wreathe atop a crown of saintly flowers.

The soul of Beauty is a part of God—
An ether through creation blown abroad :
Exhaustless : through the universe poured free—
Eternal as His own divinity.

Sweet Beauty, mother of the midnight stars,
Pours light and hope into the darkest hours ;
E'en pinks the rose above the ghastly skull,
And makes the fangs of deadliest sorrow dull.

Take Beauty from the jeweled rim of Earth,
And man will curse the hour that gave him birth ;
Exile it from the hallowed coast of Heaven,
And every hope we cherish here is riven,—
Eternity will surge a sea of gall,
E'en God Himself prepare His funeral pall.

DOLLIE HARRIS.

A true story of the invasion of Pennsylvania by the Confederate army
in 1863.

No more the cannons furrow deep
The mould wherein our fathers sleep ;
The meteor flare of sunlit sword
No more lights up the bloody sward ;
The beat of hoof and battle-yell
No more affrighten hill and dell ;
The right has won, the conflict's past,
And peace serene is ours at last.

Now we delight at fall of night
To gather 'round our firesides bright,
And list to glorious battle-rhymes,
Or read the tale of iron times.
For martial is the human heart,
And never will from valor part—
In peace we deck our battlefields,
And burnish our forefathers' shields.

'Twas on a sunny day in June,
  And wearing through the afternoon,
That General Pickett, under Lee,
Led up his Southern chivalry
Through old Greencastle's loyal town ;
And "stars and bars" and bayonets shone,
When out ran Dollie Harris true,
Wrapped in the old *red, white and blue.*

One hand lay hidden in a fold
And clasped a dagger in its hold.
"Come, tear this from my loins," she said —
"The wretch that dares it—he is dead !
Vile traitors to your fathers' trust,
You should long since have bit the dust.
Your whole curs'd army I defy,
And I shall scorn you till I die !"

She flung aback her tangled hair,
Her eyes put on an angry glare ;
The pendant portion of her flag
She shook, and sneered the "rebel rag."
Louder she shouted in her wrath,
"Why do you seem to shun my path?
Come, take the flag you have betrayed,—
Rebellious horde, you are afraid !"

"HALT !" said the Southern general, "HALT !
Return salute for such assault !
Present arms! — She's a noble maid,—
A true American," he said.
Five thousand rifles glittered clear,
Five thousand men sent up a cheer
For her, the bravest of the brave,
Unawed by prison-cell or grave.

"Forward, once more !" brave Pickett cried,—
"Such girl should be our nation's pride,
And ever hold a lofty place
In the proud annals of her race !"

Then as the heavy ranks moved on,
With bayonets slanted in the sun,
A many a Southern hero gazed
On that young woman's face amazed.

An hour brave Dollie Harris stood,
Draped in her country's flag, and viewed
The massive columns passing by,
With proud contempt and flashing eye.
Was ever braver woman born
A nation's record to adorn?
Is there no place for Dollie's name
On Pennsylvania's roll of fame?

LYRICS.

CAROLINE OF LORNE.

FIRST BALLAD.

His boat was down the river borne,
    By groves and fields of grain ;
A league below lay merry Lorne,
    The village of the plain.
The bells within the steeples rang
    A symphony divine,
While thus our swain enraptured sang
    Of his love, Caroline :

I wish I had a palace fair,
    With shining towers bedecked,
And inner walls of jasper clear,
    With beryls and rubies flecked ;
While from its floors of marble white
    Should fountains spring and chime,
Like Memnon erst to morning light,
    Or words in pleasant rhyme.

Its stately shadow-lines should cross
    A myrtle-bordered stream,
Whose quiet waves like silken floss
    Reflect the morning beam ;
And windows from its walls should peer,
    That my true love and I
Might list the song of gondolier,
    Or lovers passing by.

Here should my harp at evenfall
    Thrum to an ear divine ;
For Caroline is queen of all,
    And Caroline is mine !—

A gem amid a radiant scene,
    She shall delight the morn—
To-morrow I will wed my queen,
    And she her king in Lorne.

SECOND BALLAD.

The night had settled o'er the plain,
    And dewed the growing corn,
When in the stillness our young swain
    Came up from steepled Lorne.
The listening stars with torches bright
    Convened the heavens along,
As mournfully to the soul of night
    He sang this bitter song :

Oh for a cavern dark and deep
    In some deserted hill,
Where scarlet Autumn sears the steep,
    Or pours the smoky rill !
My choice would be a dreary wild
    On far Sierra's chain,
Where, unseen, Sorrow's smitten child
    Might shed his tears like rain.

Mine be a place where woman's face
    Ne'er wears its fickle smile,
Nor siren voice with mimic grace
    Emits its honeyed guile.
There would I tell my woes and pains
    To rocky waste and wood,
Firm in the faith that woman's veins
    Are filled with treacherous blood.

And there I'd woo the balm of death,
    Life's mad tumult to lull,
Where none might note my dying breath,
    Nor mass my parted soul.
Oh would that I had never been,
    Or she had ne'er been born ;
So I had never heard or seen
    False Caroline of Lorne !

THE PEACEFUL GLEN.

A brooklet through a peaceful glen
  Ran twinkling clear and slow,
And tuneful shepherds watched their flocks
  Along its banks below.
We walked beneath the birches sweet,
  My Mary dear and I,
What time the sun with royal hues
  Floods all the western sky.

With soft refrain the sparrow gay
  Sat in her flowery den ;
The green glade had its spreckled lark,
  The wood its jingling wren.
We strayed through ferns by tinkling falls,
  My Mary dear and I—
Oh, when the heart o'erflows with love
  How fast the moments fly !

A ship upon a stormy sea
  With foam and vapor gray,
A tearful eye and heavy heart,
  And Mary far away !
My feet upon a foreign land ;
  A vessel drifting home :
A joyous view of native shore,
  Once more in cheerful bloom.

The brooklet through the peaceful glen
  Still rippled clear and slow,
And tuneful shepherds watched their flocks
  Along its banks below.
I sought my Mary in the glen,
  Remembering pleasures fled :
They showed me there a grassy tomb,
  And told me she was dead.

My heart lies with her evermore,
  There in the silent clay,

Where daisies deck the tufted green,
And cowslips blossom gay ;
And daily there do I repair
When gloaming glooms the lea ;
And memory's angel sad and sweet
Doth walk and talk with me.

JUNIATA.

I move my boat from mooring
  On the river of my home :
From this valley so alluring,
  I shall turn no more to roam ;
For its waters are the clearest,
And its maidens are the fairest,—
Ay, and one of them the dearest
    That mine eyes have ever seen.
      Tallyho, sweet Juniata !
      I am rowing to my queen :
          Tallyho !
        Sing jolly, O,
        Juni—Juniata !

Sunset now its gold is flinging
  O'er the dancing waves elate ;
And I hear a maiden singing
  By a lilac-shaded gate ;
And the lay to me is sweeter
Than the flow of Eastern metre,
Or the chimes of great St. Peter
    To the beaded saint of Rome.
      Tallyho, sweet Juniata !
      For I near my Jennie's home,
          And I call,
        Ho, tallyho !
        Juni—Juniata !

MABEL CLARE.

Beside the Hudson's noble stream
  Dwells our good Mabel Clare,
With violet eyes and wine-red cheeks,
  And billowy bronzen hair.
She loveth man—she loveth God—
  Loveth with all her heart ;
And we who know her virtue well,
  Aver she needs no art.

She bindeth all our hearts to her
  With that love-spangled braid
Which Goodness on Affection's loom
  Weaves never to break or fade.
A simple maiden undisguised,
  Noble, and pure, and fair,
She walketh in the light of heaven,
  The one sweet Mabel Clare.

And so we love her not alone
  For sake of violet eyes,
For graceful form and angel face
  Designed for Paradise,
But for those graces of the heart
  God gives to make her rare—
To make her in her native vale
  Resistless Mabel Clare.

How blest art thou, O Hudson grand,
  Broad sweeping to the sea,
That one so pure and beautiful
  Sings loyal songs to thee.
Above the artful pride of queens
  And all their diamond glare,
Shines out the soul-attracting light
  Of glorious Mabel Clare.

FAREWELL, POTOMAC SIDE.

Farewell, sweet valley—fare-thee-well,
　　Where first the sweets of life 1 knew ;
Farewell, each walnut-shaded dell,
　　And hill and brooklet bonny blue.
Clarinda cares no more for me ;
　　Her fickle heart is dead in pride :
Farewell, farewell eternally,
　　Beloved Potomac side.

The mountain breath is in thy trees,
　　Thy willows swoon with gentle sigh ;
The young lambs cry on grassy leas,
　　And plovers flute along the sky :
Even Clarinda's mellow song
　　Rings heartsome o'er the silver tide,
But only barbs the dart of wrong—
　　Farewell, Potomac side.

While here the farmer cheers his team,
　　Or anglers tread the reedy shore,
Far from this vale and cherished stream
　　My steps shall wander evermore.
O daughter of Virginia fair,
　　My sweet, my proud inconstant bride,
Here's for thy perjury a tear !
　　Farewell, Potomac side.

1 have to-day the barb and thorn,
　　The cypress and the bitter rue ;
And thine are all the wine and corn,
　　The scented myrrh, and roses too.
But can the Heavens long forget
　　The arrow in the bleeding side ?
1 drink my cup with sad regret—
　　Farewell, Potomac side !

ANTIETAM SIDE.

How pleasant the vale where the rippling Antietam
  Salutes her green shores with a song of good will,
For there mid the bowers of wild blooming flowers
  Fair Rhoda looks out on the flume and the mill.

Young Henry she loved with a true heart's devotion,
  In the beautiful dew-spangled Summers of yore ;
But the bugles of war from the borders afar
  Called her lover away from her arms evermore.

Though lonely he sleeps in the land of the foeman,
  There is one who will never forget him at home,
Whose bosom will fret with a tender regret
  Till the roses blow over her own silent tomb.

Oh, sad is the scene when at twilight she wanders
  By the side of the star-sprinkled water alone,
Or tunes her guitar by the moon's silver car,
  And sings of a hope that has faded and gone.

Thus often must perish the fruit in the blossom,
  And the hopes of our youthhood commingle with doom,
But sweet is the faith that points upward and saith,
  The Lord will restore what is lost in the tomb.

MONOCACY WATER.

As fair as Euphrates or Pison of old,
  Which once in the bosom of Paradise rolled,
Monocacy flows through a land I love well,
  And laughs by the home of sweet Caroline Bell.

The vale of Avoca was dear unto Moore,
  And dear unto Burns was the Afton so pure,
But dearer to me is Monocacy's swell,
  And the willow-veiled cottage of Caroline Bell.

The sweetest of roses unfold in the Spring;
The sweetest of birds in the thorn-bushes sing:
The fairest of maids by Monocacy dwell,
And the queen of them all is sweet Caroline Bell.

NESCUTUNGA RIVER.

In the warm land of the West—
  In a place of prairie roses,
With her two hands on her breast,
  Cold in death my love reposes.
Oh how wild my grief for her,
  Tall and beautiful Kiunga,
Sister of the evening star
  Shining on the Nescutunga.

Near her grave the wild deer drinks
  With his brown mate from the river,
Looking up and looking down,
  Scents he hound and hunter never.
Wild the hills and plains around,
  Wild, like beautiful Kiunga,
Sister of the evening star
  Sinking o'er the Nescutunga.

Lo, the evening shadow falls;
  Hill and plain are shrouded under,
And across my darling's tomb
  Melancholy breezes wander.
Spirits, lead me to my love,
  To my heart-enshrined Kiunga,
Sister of the evening star
  Vanished from the Nescutunga.

Let me die before the morn;
  Give me my eternal pillow;
Cover me with nature's robe;
  Plant the ever-mourning willow.
Then shall I be free from pain,
  Resting with my sweet Kiunga,
Sister of the evening star
  Hidden from the Nescutunga.

THE ALLEGHANY LILY.

A THRENODY.

I know a pretty valley
 With a clear-bosom'd river,
A village from the hillside
 Seeth it forever.
And there abides a maiden,
 A sweet valley lily,
That shall ne'er lack a shelter
 When the frost cometh chilly,—
 The frost cometh chilly,
 The frost cometh chilly,
That shall ne'er lack a shelter
 When the frost cometh chilly.

Oh the grand Alleghany
 Is a dear sunny river,
And it flows by the dwelling
 Of my darling ever.
Oh, the sun gilds the waters,
 And doth shine on the lily
That shall ne'er lack a shelter
 When the frost cometh chilly,—
 The frost cometh chilly,
 The frost cometh chilly,
That shall ne'er lack a shelter
 When the frost cometh chilly.

There is no other valley
 In the wide world so winning
As the home of my people,
 Where my life had beginning,
And where the Alleghany
 Waves greeting to the lily
That shall ne'er lack a shelter
 When the frost cometh chilly,—
 The frost cometh chilly,
 The frost cometh chilly,
That shall ne'er lack a shelter
 When the frost cometh chilly.

CONESTOGA.

Through green and gold and shadow-glooms
　The Conestoga flows,
And mirrored in his silver heart
　The dome of heaven glows.
Lo, where his peaceful current cheers
　The richly wheated vale,
Amidst the landscape beautiful,
　Dwells my sweet Abigail.

It were a scene might charm a king
　At tender evenfall,
To see her tripping through the flowers,
　And hear her madrigal.
The child of light and purity,
　O'er sin she doth prevail,
And precious in the sight of Heaven
　Is my sweet Abigail.

Of all the dear enchanting things
　Descended from above,
The radiant gem outshining all
　Is Abigail, my love.
Of all the rare bewitching queens
　The peace of men assail,
Successfully outwitting all
　Stands royal Abigail.

No jewels deck her pearly neck,
　Or on her bosom shine ;
The charms that nature gave to her
　Are treasures more divine.
O Conestoga beautiful,
　May thy source never fail,
And angels guard with tender care
　Thy sweet swan, Abigail !

HAZEL GREENE.

I know a land dear to my heart
As freedom to the fawn,
Which from my memory ne'er shall part,
While life in me lives on.
And there the Lehigh, broad and bright,
Doth pour his glimmering sheen
Down through a vale of love and light,
Saluting Hazel Greene.

Around her quiet cottage home
Sleek herds in shadows drowse,
And meadow pink, and daisy bloom,
And asphodel and rose.
And there amid an ancient grove
High gleams a chapel vane,
And choristers sing God's high love
With saintly Hazel Greene.

Now down the mead her nimble feet
Light-tripping stir the dew ;
And nymph-like in this Arcady
She sings to me and you.
A basket with wild flowers in it
She bears with artless mien ;
In soft blue gown and jaunty hat,—
God bless our Hazel Greene !

No marquis, duke, nor titled earl
Walks in her suitors' train ;
But those who love the farmer-girl
Are Nature's noblemen.
No Northern empress sable-robed,
Nor jeweled Southern queen,
Can dare compare with her so rare,
God's own sweet Hazel Greene.

OLD WOODS BY THE LEHIGH RIVER.

Where splendors gild melodious days,
    And groves and fields with blossoms shine,
Where the soft wind's faint spirit strays
    Through fragrant branch and wild woodbine,
My heart still lives with my sweet Maude,
    Still hears the bells at gloaming quiver,
And flood with echoes circling broad
    The old woods by the Lehigh River.

Still through the sylvan scene I stray,
    As in the days of long ago,
When fleeting life was in its May,
    And all the stars of hope aglow.
The glory of departed hours
    Shall o'er these waters shine forever,
And Memory strew with holy flowers
    The old woods by the Lehigh River.

In other climes the groves may sleep
    At misty morn or drowsy noon,
And dead bells hang in silence deep
    In towers glimmering to the moon ;
But here one endless round invites
    To hope and joy enchanting ever,
For Memory's torch eternal lights
    The old woods by the Lehigh River.

SWANS ON THE MONEE.

Swans on the Monee chanting ha, ha !
    Swans on the Monee blue ;
But a grander music, ha, ha !
    Rings from the lips of Prue,
As she stands knee-deep in flowers
    Wet with the prairie dew.

Chorus : Swans on the Monee chanting ha, ha !
        Swans on the Monee blue,
        A man without a sweetheart, ha, ha !
        What, oh what would he do ?

Swans on the Monee chanting ha, ha !
Swans on the river blue :
Surely man were wretched, ha, ha !
Lorn of the woman true ;
Thorns would grow in the crown of pleasure,
Just as our Maker knew.

Swans on the Monee chanting ha, ha !
Swans on the river blue :
Here's to lovely woman, ha, ha !
Gentle, and kind, and true—
The richest gift received of Heaven—
Each proud man's darling Prue.

Swans on the Monee chanting ha, ha !
Swans on the river blue :
Raise the mighty anthem, ha, ha !
High as the heavens blue,
Praise the Lord for the great gift Woman,
Sweet as the morning new.

ANNIE NILL, THE RIVER GRACE.

A Song of the Rappahannock.

Through a land rich and lovely, where the wild lily grows,
The Rappahannock river in his rare beauty flows ;
And the maids of Virginia, renowned for their worth,
As they dance on his borders are the pride of the South.

Over Earth you may wander—go wander where you will,
You'll never find a sweeter than my own Annie Nill.
Her eyes are like the dewdrops that sparkle in the rose,
And the birds start a-singing wherever she goes.

Her voice is low and mellow like a flute on the sea,
And no queen o'er the ocean could be so dear to me.
With me the storm is silent, the calm is full of bliss,
E'en the sun shines at midnight wherever Annie is.

Her hair is like the mist-whorls rolling down the hill,
Shimmering in the moonlight when the dim world is still,
So fluffy, soft and silken, blown in the Summer breeze,—
My Annie is an angel that charmeth whom she please.

There is on Earth a Heaven wherever Annie smiles ;
There's not a trace of evil in her sweet winning wiles :
The sun shines at midnight—it's ever, ever morn
Where Annie scatters favors, for a new time is born !

The Rappahannock river upon his shores of green
Has just as lovely maidens as the round world has seen ;
And there my heart forever will crave a biding-place
With Annie Nill, my darling, the witching *River Grace.*

JOHNNY-JUMP-UPS.

A Child's Song.

Lovingly inscribed to Nona May Kettoman.

Little johnny-jump-ups,
    Twenty in a row ;
Twenty little blue caps,
    What a pretty show !
Merry little fellows,
    Dancing in the sun,
Telling us of better days,
    Sunny hours and fun.

Chorus : Little johnny-jump-ups,
    All in loyal blue,
You look always up to heaven,
    Just as I should do.

Little johnny-jump-ups,
    Early in the Spring,
With the sweet arbutus,
    When the robins sing
Heartsome little anthems
    That sweet memories bring,
Lift you up your pretty heads
    To hear the brambles ring.

Little johnny-jump-ups,
    You are dainty flowers,
Pretty blue-eyed children
    Of the April showers ;
And you come to cheer us
    In the barren hours
That precede the Summer-tide
    With the prouder flowers.

A DAWN CAROL.

Now smiles the chaste and holy Dawn
    On herbs and flowers springing,
And wakes to play the spotted fawn,
    And starts the birds a-singing.

I see her playfully in the rills
    Her trailing garments dipping,
Then up the coral Eastern hills
    On golden sandals tripping.

Sweet innocence smiles in her face,
    Her visage fair adorning,
As praising God with songs of grace
    She leads the saintly morning.

Gladly the poet hails her star
    Above his native mountains,
And sees its image from afar
    Endiamonding the fountains :

And he goes forth with sounding strings
    To meet the angel coming,
While many a bee and wild bird sings
    Responsive to his thrumming.

It minds him of his coming Lord,
    Glories supreme adorning,
When Christ shall to His saints award
    The grand, eternal morning.

LAND OF THE SAINTS THAT ARE DEAD.

In Memory of M. E. K.

I know that the scene is exceedingly fair,
And the attars of Paradise sweeten the air;
I know the great King in His glory is there,
    In the Land of the Saints that are Dead.

The hope of all hopes, satisfying and sweet,
Is the one that assures me I some day shall meet
With the loved I have lost, in an Eden complete,
    In the Land of the Saints that are Dead.

Pale Sorrow may sadly suppress every smile,
And the snares of the Evil One lure me to guile,
But the triumph of striving will come after while,
    In the Land of the Saints that are Dead.

Oh sweet after toil will be heavenly rest—
How grand to the soul that has long been distressed,
The harp and the crown and the songs of the Blest,
    In the Land of the Saints that are Dead.

Long, long have I mourned for my child in the tomb,
Now the promise of Jesus disperses my gloom;
The rose that here faded hath exquisite bloom
    In the Land of the Saints that are Dead.

I'll not wish him back in this sad world again,
Where the bliss of true loving is mingled with pain;
Ah, surely more happy are spirits that reign
    In the Land of the Saints that are Dead.

I am nearing the end of my journey, I know;
I have suffered and hoped—I am ready to go,
Across the white stream in the valley below,
    To the Land of the Saints that are Dead.

A SWEET MADRIGAL.

Young Maud she is a bonnie girl,
(Oh, the shrub in the mere is thorning !)
Her hair flows down in tuft and whorl,
When the wind blows cool in the morning.

Man were undone to dwell alone,
(Oh, the shrub in the mere is thorning !)
So I must make sweet Maud my own,
When the wind blows cool in the morning.

Oh blissful day when her I wed,
(Oh, the shrub in the mere is thorning !)
And kiss her cheeks to crimson-red,
When the wind blows cool in the morning.

But better still our love will show,
(Oh, the shrub in the mere is thorning !)
When hand in hand seaward we go,
And the wind blows cool in the morning.

And grandest of all the sight will be,
(Oh, the shrub in the mere is thorning !)
When we've together crossed the sea,
And the wind blows cool in the morning.

True love is more than bridal kiss,
(Oh, the shrub in the mere is thorning !)
It should reach into Heaven's bliss,
When the wind blows cool in the morning.

LILLITH.

Lillith, Lillith—
How my heart thrilleth
With the love of Lillith !
The sky blueth,
The dove cooeth,
The lark singeth,
The dingle ringeth,
The bee hummeth,
The heart drummeth
When Lillith cometh !

Light she bringeth,
　And music, too ;
And the song she singeth
　Is pure as dew.
She decketh the day
With an olive spray,
And the brow of night
With a braid of light.
She maketh the Winter
　Warm like Summer ;
Oh rare is the magic
　Of this new comer !

There is no sorrow
　Where Lillith is ;
And each rare to-morrow
　Bringeth us new bliss,
Till from pain we borrow
　A sweet surcease.

The rich sunshine
　Of her Summery soul,
Like a balm divine,
　Maketh all heart-whole.
Lillith, Lillith—
How my heart thrilleth
With the love of Lillith !

NIOBRARAH.

The Englishman extols the Thames,
　The Scotchman Doon and Yarrow,
But, oh, a dearer stream to me
　Is our wild Niobrarah !

There sings the yellow-billed cuckoo,
　And pipes the scarlet sparrow,
And prairie flowers lean to see
　Themselves in Niobrarah.

But sweeter far than these to me,
  The settler's daughter, Clara,
Dwells in the mellow light of heaven
  That falls on Niobrarah.

Her beauty charms the Indian brave,
  She feareth not his arrow ;
He calls her " *White Swan*," and he smiles
  On her from Niobrarah.

'Tis true her father is not great,
  His fields are short and narrow ;
But, oh, his honest heart is grand
  And broad as Niobrarah.

From morn till night he binds the sheaf,
  Or draws the fertile furrow ;
No time is there for pomp or pride
  Beside the Niobrarah.

Give princesses to dukes and kings,
  But give me my love Clara,
And I will be as blest as they,
  And dwell by Niobrarah.

THE OLD HOME PLACE.

A Song.

  I have wandered far and wide,
  Over land and over tide,
I have gazed on the rarest of grace,
  But I've found no other spot
  With so much of beauty fraught
  As the kingdom of my childhood,
    The Old Home Place.

Chorus : The Old Home Place
      With its violets so blue,
    The Old Home Place
      With its hearts so leal and true ;
    The pride of my father,
    The home of my mother,
    My sister and my brother—
Heaven breathe a blessing on the Old Home Place !

I have lingered half the year
Where the roses of Cashmere
Were magnificent in odor and grace,
But more beautiful to me
Seem the lilies on the lea,
In the kingdom of my childhood,
The Old Home Place.

I have felt what man doth feel
When cathedral organs peal
Under domes where angel-wings interlace ;
But a grander melody
Seems the Sabbath psalm to me,
In the kingdom of my childhood,
The Old Home Place.

When I die I will not ask
Sculptured tomb or obelisk :
Let them lay me down with tenderness and grace
Where the violets will blue
In the summer sun and dew,
In the kingdom of my childhood,
The Old Home Place.

IRISH LINEN.

NOTE.—In the time of my boyhood it was a common occurrence to see Irish peddlers roaming over the country selling towels, table-cloths and handkerchiefs, generally asserting that they were brought with them from their fathers' farms. Of course modern license laws have made this avocation a thing of the past.

BALLAD.

Come, buy towels and table-cloths,
All of Irish linen, O !
Father broke and scutched the flax,
Mother did the spinnin', O !
My good sister reeled the yarn ;
Brother cast the shuttle, O !
Oft I've sat beside his loom
Listening to its rattle, O !

Chorus: Come, buy Irish linen, O !
 Sixteen-hundred linen, O !
 White as swans on dear Lough Neagh,
 Mother did the spinnin', O !

Near Armagh where I was born
 All the folks wear linen, O !
All the men are dressing flax,
 All the women spinnin', O !
Shamrock green and Irish flax,
 Side by side they flourish, O !
All around the "praties" bloom,
 Irish hearts to nourish, O !

Och, to see them handle flax—
 Pull, and dry, and break it, O !
Smite it with the scutching knife,
 Through the heckle rake it, O !
See them spin it into thread,
 Reel and knot it singin', O !
Weave it into fabric fine—
 Bleach the Irish linen, O !

Come, buy Irish linen fine,
 Brought across the ocean, O !
From the greenest island rolled
 'Round with Earth in motion, O !
God be with that land oppressed,
 Still to fond hopes clingin', O !
Come, buy of her wandering son
 Treasures of her linen, O !

MAUDE OF TUCKAHOE.

In wandering up and down this world,
 And roving to and fro,
I fell in love with a sweet girl
 In pious Tuckahoe,
Where churches stand on every hand,
 And bells ring loud and slow.

Chorus: O Maude of Tuckahoe,
Sweet Maude of Tuckahoe,
If I had twenty wives to win
I'd woo in Tuckahoe !

The river like a golden braid
Lay glimmering in the green,
And fragrant shrubs and nodding reeds
Across the pools did lean,
When charming Maude walked out abroad
Amid the lovely scene.

I saw her in her scarlet gown,
With rosy cheeks aglow ;
My heart cast out its iron hates,
And love began to grow ;
So now I stay till life's last day
With Maude of Tuckahoe.

O Maude of Tuckahoe,
Sweet Maude of Tuckahoe,
If I had twenty wives to win
I'd woo in Tuckahoe !

BEAUTIFUL MONONGAHELA.

Beautiful Monongahela,
Loveliest river of the west,
With thy daisy-spangled borders,
And the heavens in thy breast !
Thou shalt never be forgotten
Wheresoe'er on Earth I roam ;
Aye my heart goes back to bless thee,
River of my childhood home.

In thy windy elms rocking
Still the black-eyed robins sing,
And the goldfinch weaves her hammock
In the saffron-scented Spring.
Still the cloud-enamored plover
Flutes above thee, long and wild,
Serenading Heaven's windows,
Just as when I was a child.

Lowing cattle crop thy meadows
  Where the spreckled lily grows,
And the lamb lies down to slumber
  In the shadow of the rose.
Mill and cottage throw their shadows
  Still across thy sandy bed,
And the eye-delighting rainbow
  Builds her bright bridge overhead.

Beautiful Monongahela,
  Sweet queen river of the west,
With my people on thy borders,
  And the heavens in thy breast !
On thy banks I wish to slumber,
  With thy waters murmuring near,
When I pass into the shadow
  Of the grave's unending year.

THE SUSQUEHANNA LOVER.

A Passionate Song.

Along the Susquehanna's banks
  A happy lover strayed,
And thus he sang adoringly
  The charms of some sweet maid :

My love is like a fruitful land
  That Heaven hath greatly blest,—
A store of riches manifold,
  In tempting beauty drest.

Her eyes do match the star that shines
  Just after set of sun ;
Her cheeks are like twin roses are
  When day has just begun.

Her voice is like a silver flute
  Played on a moonlit sea,
When every note is pregnant with
  The soul of melody.

She's stately as yon slender ash
   That by the river grows,
Her countenance is like the morn
   Coming to pink the rose.

By day she is my radiant sun,
   My dream-star in the night ;
And never shall an earthly gem
   Astrange from her my sight.

From virtue's pathway beautiful
   Her steps have never strayed ;
The holy love she giveth me
   Shall never be betrayed.

FOR AYE AND AYE.

I met my love in a shady nook,
   In the golden Summer-tide ;
She held in her hand a spangled book,
   With fair leaves open wide.
I saw therein a sweet refrain,
   In an old-time roundelay,
At every close I read it plain,
   " Sweetheart, for aye and aye,
      For aye and aye,
Sweetheart, for aye and aye."

I said, "The years may come and go
   With sunshine, dear, and rain,
With Summer rose and Winter snow,
   And seasons of joy and pain ;
But love atween us should not die,
   Nor ever know decay ;
We should be lovers, you and I,
   Sweetheart, for aye and aye,
      For aye and aye,
Sweetheart, for aye and aye !"

She laid her warm white hand in mine,
  And thus made sweet reply :
" Whate'er betide, my heart is thine,
  And fear not, though I die,
My spirit still will steadfast prove
  When far from earth away—
In depths of woe, or vales of love,—
  Sweetheart, for aye and aye,
      For aye and aye,
  Sweetheart, for aye and aye."

I said, " My true love, this I vow,
  While endless ages run,
Though death be white upon my brow,
  My soul and thine are one.
Though green grass waves above our graves
  All the long Summer day,
I will be thine if thou'lt be mine,
  Sweetheart, for aye and aye,
      For aye and aye."
She answered, looking up to God,
  " Sweetheart, for aye and aye ! "

MARGUERITE.

Water-lilies in the bay
Still are laughing all the day,
Where the stately shadows fall
Down from tower, and tree, and wall ;
And the birds still carol sweet
Where the woods and waters meet ;
But the maiden Marguerite
Rides no more the ripples bright,
And her boat against the shore
Rocks at anchor evermore.

Still the grey ships come and go
Through the foam as white as snow,
And the breeze comes up the lea
From the crystal-breasted sea ;

And the sun shines all the day
Over rock, and wood, and bay,
But sweet Marguerite is gone
From the breezy bay and lawn,
And her white boat by the shore
Rocks at anchor evermore.

Sweetest flower in dust is laid :
Marguerite the pure is dead.
In the charnel-vault she lies,
With the death-sleep in her eyes,
And her white hands on her breast
Crossed in everlasting rest ;
But her pure soul, far away,
Dwells in realms of endless day,
And her boat against the shore
Rocks at anchor evermore.

EDNA.

A Song.

Edna, Edna,—
The pale moon sifteth her silver dust
  Over the shadowy woods and town ;
Angels sent to number the just
  On a drowsy world look down,
    And their lamps I see
    As I come to thee,
        Edna, Edna.

Edna, Edna—
Sweet Love is my heartsome theme to-night,
  The sweetest of themes in this good broad world :
Thou art my hope, and thou my light,
  However the clouds be curled :
    When thine eyes I see
    There is light for me,
        Edna, Edna.

Edna, Edna,
When thy gentle heart beats close to mine,
Exquisite, indeed, is the bliss I feel ;
Softly and tightly our arms entwine,
While the long-drawn kiss I steal :
And the sting of thy kiss
Is sweeter than bliss !
Edna, Edna.

A PASTORAL SONG.

How softly purl the lullsome rills
Between their banks of green,
While singing winds run up the hills
The streams run down between.
But purling brooks and singing winds
Had dearth of melody,
Were not my love in this same grove,
To listen them with me.

And neither would the flowers please,
Nor any spice be sweet,
And all the birds that charm the trees
As well might find retreat.
Without her fond, approving smile
Myself would silent be,
And everything designed to please
Become a mockery.

Oh, if she turn away from me,
And like a stranger go,
A ghoul were heard in every bird,
And flowers were food for woe.
Yea, all sweet things were turned to gall,
And radiant day to night ;
And who would care to live at all
Exiled from each delight.

MY OWN COUNTRY.

The soft wind blows, the ruffled rose
  Is drooping in the vale ;
The fragrant flowers of woodbine bowers
  Perfume the cooling gale.
Earth's flowers may bloom awhile for some,
  But never more for me !
Life's sun is low, and I must go
  Home to my own country.

Oh, sweet and fair the flowers there;
  They wither not like here ;
One Spring for aye—one endless day—
  And leaves turn never sere.
Oh, pure are all the streams that roll
  Adown the Heavenly lea ;
No pain or gloom can ever come
  Into my own country.

Why would I live? Why should I grieve
  Longer in this strange land,
Since I may tread the streets o'erspread
  With gold by my Lord's hand?
Adieu, adieu, sweet friends, to you—
  Would you could go with me
To walk the streets and taste the sweets
  That bless my own country.

Oh, stay not long when I am gone,
  Come over soon to me :
You're welcome where the blest ones are,
  Come to my own country !
Earth's flowers may bloom awhile for some,
  But now no more for me :
Life's sun is low, and I must go
  Home to my own country.

WATERS O' THE AYR.

Of a' the pleasant streams that glide
  Down highlan's grand and green,
Or thro' the lowlan's swim in pride,
  Fringed wi' a flowery scene,
There's nane tae me sae pure an' sweet—
  There's nane ye can compare
Wi' that that laved my boyhood feet,
  The waters o' the Ayr.

There Robie Burns in lang-gane days
  Loud whistled tae the dawn,
Or saft amang the cowslip braes
  Sang when the sun was gone,
Such songs as still start love's sweet flame,
  An' dow na' find compare
In ony lan' that canna claim
  The waters o' the Ayr.

Now I wad gie a hundred pound
  To-day an' it were mine,
Could I but view that sacred ground
  As in sweet years lang syne ;
And meet my lassie mid the flowers,
  My lassie, oh, sae fair,
Where wimple under woodbine bowers
  The waters o' the Ayr.

JEAN ANDERSON MY DEAR.

REPLY TO JOHN ANDERSON MY JO.

Jean Anderson, my dear Jean,
  Sit closer up to me ;
Tae hear ye speak so kindly,
  Much pleasure doth me gie.
'Tis true yo're nae sae lythe, Jean,
  As when my bride ye were,
But ye're the same kind saul tae me,
  Jean Anderson my dear.

Jean Anderson, my dear Jean,
  Twice thretty Springs we've seen,
And a' our leal guid frens in youth
  Lie in the kirkyard green.
And we maun soon gae too, Jean ;
  I seem tae see frae here
Twa friendly slabs aneath the hill,
  Jean Anderson my dear.

TRIXIE.

Fair, black-eyed Trixie is a girl
  Whom any one must love ;
Yet she is not angel, nor
  A sinless turtle-dove.
Her roguish eyes are merciless—
  Of Trixie I must say
She's flavored with the mint of sin,
  And human every way.

She has a rather truant heart,—
  A little hard to catch,—
And yet I think I hold the string
  That is to lift the latch.
But I am not too sure of this,
  I have her promise not ;
And in the kettle where I stew
  She keeps the water hot !

Sometimes she's very kind to me,
  But often plays me false ;
I must confess 'twixt hope and doubt
  I sweat with rapid pulse !
Trixie's an ever-jesting minx,
  With merry, scornful laugh ;
To-day she'll feed me upon wheat,
  To-morrow upon chaff.

Her veins are blue with ancient blood :
  She is of Adam's race :
But blood of king, or duke, or lord
  Has in her veins no place.
Such rancid strain may be a prize
  Where men in bondage be,
But in this free America
  My Trixie dear for me !

THE END.

ADDENDA.

A New Poet.

We had occasion recently to visit one of the most beautiful
sections of Pennsylvania, where mountain, valley and stream
combine to create the various types of landscape so necessary to
the development of the poetical element in man's nature; and
while enjoying the peaceful quietude of a retired and unfre-
quented village, at the hospitable home of the village pastor, we
met a youth of some eighteen or twenty years, whose history
interested us greatly.

As we first saw him entering the pastor's home there was
nothing very noticeable in his appearance. Rustic and unpre-
tending in his manners and bearing, with no apparent effort to
cultivate fashion or style, the main thing we observed was that
he was a young man of thoughtful mould, earnest heart, clear
eye, and an evident fixedness of purpose. Having a roll in his
hand, he reminded us somewhat of Bunyan's portraiture of the
Pilgrim. From the estimable pastor we learned that he was a
youth of uncommon natural abilities, and after having read a
short literary production of his, were astonished at learning that
he was *entirely self-taught.*

Reared in the midst of the friendly forest which yielded his
father a scanty support, with no near neighbors and but few
friends with whom to hold intercourse, the youth grew up in
solitude, making his companions of the trees and flowers of the
mountain-side, and the crystal bounding brooks and streamlets,
and the birds who awoke him with their early matinal warbling.

With these surroundings, the tendency of most minds would
have been towards the unthinking wildness of the "gentle
savage." There was no incentive to intellectual exertion or
improvement. But it seems that the majestic works of God were
silent teachers to the thirsty soul of *this* boy. The grand scenery

that stretched in wide expanse before his view as he stood in the cottage-door seemed to stir his soul with high purposes and noble resolves. The rustling leaves and the sighing winds whispered to him the most delightful thoughts of poesy, and all of nature's handiwork brought to his eager, receptive mind views of the Divine Creator who made all things and pronounced them good.

Humanly speaking this young mind stood alone. There was no sympathetic or appreciative person at hand to draw out and develop the germ of genius which stirred within him ; and to all appearances there was no alternative but that he should, when he arrived at a sufficient age, shoulder his polished axe and follow the humble pursuit of his aged parent.

This indeed he was required to do, and he did it without complaint, but with each reverberating blow of the axe it would seem new and Heaven-sent thoughts germinated in his mind.

At night, while the aged woodchopper slept the sleep that comes only to honest toil, the boy pored over his books, endeavoring to satisfy his thirst for knowledge, and upon many a belated traveler has the light of his tallow-dip gleamed out from the little window of his attic chamber. We had an opportunity later to examine more particularly some of the works of this highly gifted youth, and we took pains to show them to friends of literary culture on our return to Philadelphia, all of whom were greatly impressed with the undoubted evidences of his genius.—EDWIN H. NEVIN, D. D., *in the Philadelphia Commercial and Manufacturers' Gazette.*

DISCOVERY OF A POET.

I am elated—whether justifiably so or not you may determine for yourself.

That it was something to detect a new continent, as Columbus did, or even Canada, as did Jacques Cartier, I don't deny ; but of infinitely more importance, in my judgment, is the first disclosure of a genuine, passionate poet ! " Who," it should be borne in mind, " but the poets first made gods for men ; brought them down to us, and raised us up to them ? " I think Emerson somewhere bears me out in this when he remarks how thrilling an event it is when a thinker is let loose upon the earth.

Thus considered, I have no doubt that Newton's revelation of the law of fluxions was a far grander achievement than the mere first glimpse that Columbus, standing on the castle of the *Santa Maria,* caught of the light burning dimly on the coasts of San Salvador. Consequently, I repeat, I am elated, for I have discovered a brand-new poet.

Where the Blue Ridge Mountain stretches its bristly backbone parallel with the Mason and Dixon's line ; where one of a steady head can stand on the outermost ledge of High Rock Peak and look down into the Cumberland Valley as into a vast amphitheatre—at Pen-Mar, which as you see is so exactly on the border-line that one must be strictly impartial and give it the initial syllable of each State—there I found him, my Axeman Bard.

My poet's name——. Let me ask you seriously if the folly of Juliet's question has ever presented itself to your mind in connection with the names of poets ? Do you not think that Hogg's indifferent success may not in large part be due to his name? Or in all earnestness do you believe Shakespeare himself would have been the same to us if his father, with the family name of Shakeskillet, had piled Pelion on Ossa by calling his son Hezekiah? Would your tongue cleave to the roof of your mouth if you had to say the "divine Shakeskillet"? At any rate my poet's name is Kettoman—George Washington Kettoman, in full. Not a heavy load to carry, and yet I fear it may handicap him.

While the "powder devilkins" from South and North were grappling in deadly wrestle on the field of Gettysburg, my poet, then a lad of ten years, lay in his father's yard beneath a spreading tree, four miles northward, all enwrapped in a pacific struggle with the English language. He was writing verse. And to the curious mind it may be of interest to inquire—of these two events, the gory, tremendous tragedy enacted about Little Round Top, or the silent commotion in the brain of this boy, which after all may time prove to have been of more permanent interest and profit to mankind? May not the simple influx of the divine inflatus into the soul of this lad, whereby he gave mental *birth* (mark you !) to his first score of metrical lines, have been a more fateful act than the slaughter of a thousand score of men in the valley below?

In his eleventh year he came to the mountains, and in the mountains he has ever since remained. When Nature selects a congenial spirit to whom she imparts her secrets, it is interesting to note that, with her confidence, she invariably bestows a gift of expression, whereby these subtle secrets may be tattled to others—to the world at large. And in this the discerning mind may observe on the part of Nature a most astonishing whimsicalness : to tell, namely, in mysterious fashion her secrets to the elect, and then endow them with the talent of telling these secrets to others. Certainly the inquiry is pertinent—why employ middlemen at all? Why not prate your secrets, O Nature ! to all of us and be done with it ?

Yet such is her freakish conduct, and perhaps the best proof I can offer you of the merit of my poet is this,—that Nature has has given him a double vehicle for the expression of the fantastic things she whispers in his ears ; not only does my poet drive a dripping quill, but he has such exceeding craft with the pencil that I am uncertain in which he is the more skillful. Thus, as he modestly tells me,—"I am able to illustrate my own poems according to my own taste, which, to say the least, is a great satisfaction."

When day had utterly died out and such gloom as one can only find in the forest had fallen about the lowly cabin, a solitary light gleamed out from the attic window, and its rays doubtless greeted the eye of many a belated traveler in the woods ; just as the heaven-born spark, kindling in the brain of the boy bent eagerly before the candle, might some day burst into a light whose rays would pierce the thick gloom around many a human heart.

What aspirations he had, even in his early boyhood, you may guess from the following :

Oh that I were an heir to fame,
In glorious thoughts and deeds abounding,
That future bards might send my name
Forever down the ages sounding.

Oh, sweet to have our lives approved,
And with the world's chief names be numbered,
And be renowned, admired and loved
When we are gone years many a hundred.

> Oh, sweet to think that then bright eyes
> Would read our life's immortal story,
> And turn in transport to the skies
> And for us thank the Lord of Glory!

*   *   *   *   *

> But to be dead without a name—
> Gone like a brute or slave from earth,
> Forgotten in a day—what pain!
> 'Twere better I had died in birth!

Do you recall that wise historical deduction of Vauvenargnes?
—"*Les plus grands ministres ont été ceux que la fortune avait placés
le plus loin du ministère.*" So may destiny have placed my poet at
the most distant point from the glory he craves; starting him on
his career, there in the mountains, forced each morning to
shoulder his axe and attack the giants of the forest, and at night
to light his tallow-dip in the frosty air of the garret and bitterly
chop his way into the heart of the tree of knowledge—all that,
like Sully or Mazarin, he might finally issue disciplined by
adversity into the full light of fame.

Thus has my self-taught Axeman Bard gone tranquilly on his
way, sure of the guerdon that awaits him at the end of his
journey.

"Like Burns," says he, "I like to celebrate in my little way
the names of our beautiful rivers,"—

> The Englishman extols the Thames.
> The Scotchman Doon and Yarrow.
> But oh! a sweeter stream to me
> Is our wild Niobrarah.

Again he sings,—

> Sunset now its gold is flinging
> O'er the dancing waves elate,
> And I hear a maiden singing
> By a lilac-shaded gate:
> And the lay to me is sweeter
> Than the flow of Eastern metre,
> Or the chimes of great St. Peter
> To the beaded saint of Rome.
>> Tallyho! sweet Juniata!
>> Glad my Jenny sings at home—
>> Sings to me—ho! Tally-ho!
>> Juni—Juniata!

And once more,—

> Near her grave the wild deer drinks
> With his brown mate from the river,
> Looking up and looking down,
> Scents he hound and hunter never.
> Wild the hills and plains around,
> Wild, like beautiful Kiunga—
> Sister of the evening star
> Sinking o'er the Nescatunga.

Even by these tokens you may agree with me that Pennsylvania can now lift her bowed head and say to the other United States,—"Sisters, jeer me no more. I am not alone prolific of petroleum and coal. Nay, Bayard Taylor and the genial obese Boker were not the last or even the best I had to show you. Behold Kettoman, the Axeman Bard!"

Tell me, can you conjure the green hue of envy that would have come into Poe's dark eyes could he have read these lines?—

> Thy voice is like the harp of God
> By angels heard in Paradise:
> Thou art replete with every sweet,
> And hast the most distracting eyes.
> O hallowed Numalore!
> Soul-thrilling Numalore!
> Are there not vows carved in the yore,
> Beauteous, brilliant Numalore?

My poet sends me a bundle of verses to read, and I find myself, after their perusal, no longer wondering in the manner of the Jews—can any good come out of a *policeman*? For I should previously have told you that of recent summers the necessity of earning his daily bread has driven my poet to keep watch over the pavilion at High Rock, where gather the pampered sons and daughters of Maryland. Fancy, then, a nineteenth century policeman bubbling over in this wise:

> Lilies, lilies, white and pure, as the robes the Holy wear
> In the halls of my good Lord, where the brides of glory are,—
> You I love, and kneeling here by this old moss-emerald wall,
> Feel regret I cannot kneel and with kiss salute you all!
> You are better than the roses, for my Saviour mentioned you,
> Proving to the sinner's mind that the words He spake were true:
> Holy flowers thus glorified,
> Cheer my grave when I have died!

Where is there another policeman like unto him? But how immeasurably removed is my poet-policeman from all others when he sings in such a strain as this :

> Vapors curl white about the moon,
> Whose pale beams fall aslant the lake ;
> Dumb Silence reigns in deep content,—
> I love her for her stillness sake !
> This dim wild time enchants my mind !
> The graves are white along the hill—
> Are white and pure as angels' thrones:
> I've loved them long—I love them still !

No one surely could recognize in a sentiment like this the prosaic hand of a protector of the peace. Did you ever know of a policeman who, on observing a "star shoot" in the heavens, would be likely in reference to the event to say :

> A meteor plowed the steel-blue skies,
> And trailed a line of fire behind . . . ?

Or on mentioning Miltiades (if, indeed, you can find another policeman who ever heard of him) to make the apt and drastic observation that

> The lily here is twisted with the thunderbolt—?

So I am persuaded that whatever your verdict may be upon the value of my discovery from a poetic point of view, you must at least grant me that I have unearthed the most remarkable policeman who "beats" upon the surface of the globe, and certainly this is something.

I have fitly reserved to the last the *crowning* peculiarity of my poet. What, or rather whom do you think he looks like?

An universal impression prevails that genuine poets should have an abundance of hair like Bryant, Longfellow, Tennyson, and Walt Whitman, who rather suggest this as an infallible test of the true virile bard and seer. Consequently a poet, even if he is not hairy, is popularly and paradoxically regarded—if you will pardon the vulgarism—as a *hairy* poet. See now how eccentric is my Axeman Bard.

His dark hair is cut short ; a modest moustache covers his firm upper lip, and—in flagrant violation of every canon relating to the external appearance of poets from Homer down to the sweet singer of Michigan—from beneath the swell of his lower lip there depends a thin *goatee* barely an inch in length. Upon the wisdom or taste of this whim I must remain mute. It hardly seems right to me that a poet should wear a goatee ; but then did not Pope wear a canvas bodice and *three* pairs of stockings?

Meanwhile the tallow-dip still gleams in the lonely cot on the saddle of the Blue Mountain, and in the winter my Axeman Bard, as his neighbors round about are calling him, deftly wields the pen and pencil with the same fingers that have gripped and stiffened all day around the handle of his axe.

And as he thus stands revealed to you through my imperfect exhibit—a hewer of wood by day, and a drawer of pictures and poems by night—tell me, what do you think of him? Have I found a Pennsylvania Burns? Shall I cry Eureka?—MELVILLE PHILIPS, *in Chicago Current.*

"DAWN."

Our Axeman Bard, Mr. Geo. W. Kettoman, illumines our first page to-day with the latest product of his gifted genius, in the shape of a sonnet upon the above theme. It came in for publication some weeks ago, and has been held over pending an opportunity on our part to give it more attention than is usually at hand for literary criticism.

*   *   *   *   *

But we started out to say that Mr. Kettoman's last effort is in his happiest style. He is always happy in nature, in the "humanities."

The majesty of the mountain cliffs that surround his humble home on the Blue Ridge—the splendors of the heavens by day and night—the storms—the weird music of the winds howling around the mountain's crest, or sighing in the gently swaying branches—the echoes ringing from rock to rock, and through the deep, dark gorges—the delicious fragrance and gentler music wafted up from the rills and brooklets that go dancing down the mountain sides—the great miracle of landscapic splendor that bewilders the eye from High Rock and Mt. Quirauk—all these have melted into the heart, and the soul, and mind of the poet, and are the rich fuel upon which the fires of his genius have fed.

Mr. Kettoman is essentially a "nature's poet." He is best in the Lyric. True, he has done good work in the Heroic also. Indeed, he demonstrates a versatility of talent and breadth of poetic nature that can successfully adapt itself to most any form of verse or poetic character. But the Lyric—the realm of beauty, of music, flowered meadows, peaceful streams, fantastic flitting of lights and shadows across the landscape, the mystic inspiration of the countless voices of nature, the ever-varying splendors of sky and landscape—here (as well as of course the realm of moral beauty—religion, love, devotion, virtue, truth, piety) is where our bard most loves to linger and tune his ever sweetening lyre.

In " Dawn," nature's most inspiriting and fascinating phenomenon, he finds a fertile field for the development of that inner love of the beautiful, that delicacy of poetic instinct, that fantastic imagery, that subtlety of treatment so characteristic of the poet and his work. It is a short poem, to be sure—just the length of a sonnet, but in it there is painting, and there is music, and the highest conception of physical beauty and magnificence ; and above all these a refined sensibility and elevated Christian tone.

The Greek idea is suggested all through, but nature is painted more familiarly to the English eye, and the thought reaches a sublimity not known to mythology. Aurora was simply the goddess beautiful, rising fresh out of the ocean every morning, and being pursued lovingly over the hills by Apollo.

To this sensualistic conception only did the Pagan idea go. But in Mr. Kettoman's Aurora we have a no less splendid conception of physical charms, but we have them presented in the highest state of excellence as "Queen of the hour of praise."

This is the dominant chord in the sonnet, and charms the Christian heart.

To us the "Dawn" has, indeed, a meaning. It is for a truth the "hour of praise." The church reflects this thought in every age and takes the first moments of the day to offer its incense of praise to Heaven. To the poet, and Christianized imagination too, all things are conceived to join in this worship.

"The hills awake ; incense and song arise," just as the poet beautifully says, and all nature swells the grand anthem of joy and thanksgiving. This is much of what gives to "Dawn" its beauty and meaning.

We love personal beauty just as much as did the ancients: love to impersonate this lovely matinal phenomenon, " Dawn," as a glorious "goddess" just as well as did the Greeks, but we love also—and more—to clothe her with spiritual attributes and functions, so that she may have a higher calling than merely posing as a thing of beauty with nothing to do but have perennial flirtations with Apollo.

We like the poem all through. It is true to nature—the first condition of art—it is light, airy, and delicate, and withal strong in touch where necessary. To the ear it is full of melody, and to the eye it reveals richest pictures. The "Gazette" is always happy when conning the divine Kettoman.—N. BRUCE MARTIN, A. M., in *Keystone Gazette*, Waynesboro, Pa.

ANNOUNCEMENT.

A FORTHCOMING PROSE WORK,

By Geo. W. KETTOMAN.

THE BEAUTIFUL ZIDONIAN;

OR,

SOLOMON'S PALACE OF PEARLS.

A Tale of the Early Orient.

Based to a great extent upon facts obtained by recent explorers, and from Sacred History, the works of Josephus, and plausible traditions and theories. Almost equivalent to a history of the life, times and exploits of Solomon, together with the same of King Hiram, Pharaoh-the-nameless, Sesonchis (Shishak) the usurper, and others of note in the days of the wise king; with scenes laid in Memphis, Tyre, Jerusalem, Forest of Lebanon, and Tadmor, called also the city of perfumes, owing to the fact that it could be smelled for miles in the soft winds of the Syro-Arabian desert, the odor emanating from its numerous perfume factories and bazars of fragrant oils.

Solomon, the central figure in this work, was the greatest king, merchant, scientific author, preacher, poet and lover the world has ever known. His life was therefore richer in romance than that of any other. Apropos, he received more valuable gifts in a single year than all other sovereigns taken together in six thousand years!

This book attempts to show us this intellectual giant in love. What a field for a proper pen!

It is a book of iron hates and golden loves, of atrocious cruelties and tender sympathies,—a book of truth, and yet a fiction ; a book of science, and withal a romance.

A beautiful and accomplished Zidonian princess, who in childhood was ensconced in the brilliant court of Hiram, King of Tyre, of which she soon became the flower and light, is our heroine. She attracted the attention of Solomon, the friend of Hiram, and he conceived an almost uncontrollable affection for her ; but had a formidable rival in the person of a Jewish shepherd, who saved her from the jaws of a lion in the wilderness of Lebanon. Having founded the magnificent city of Tadmor, Solomon made the fair Zidonian its first queen, presenting her with the wonderful and costly "Palace of Pearls." Rissennah was the first and Zenobia the last queen of this splendid and opulent city.

The friends of *Masonry* will find in this book something interesting regarding the ancient "Tyrian Order of the Circle and Angle."

Solomon is believed to have finished his education at the "Kings' College" in Memphis (Noph), where, most likely, he met the daughter of Pharaoh whom he married. At this same school (where Geometry was invented) in later days Pythagoras received the knowledge of the "True System of the World."

Price of the book, illustrated and bound in gold and crimson cloth, $1.25. In paper cover, 75 cents.

Will be sold to subscribers only and limited to their demand.

Books payable on delivery.

Order early, addressing

GEO. W. KETTOMAN,

HIGHFIELD, MD.

www.ingramcontent.com/pod-product-compliance
Lightning Source LLC
Chambersburg PA
CBHW032204010726
47493CB00008BA/2830